Match Me If You Can

Match Me If You Can

Tiana Smith

Swoon READS

Swoon Reads
New York

A Swoon Reads Book

An imprint of Feiwel and Friends and Macmillan Publishing Group, LLC

175 Fifth Avenue, New York, NY 10010

Our books may be purchased in bulk for promotional, educational, or business use. Please contact your local bookseller or the Macmillan Corporate and Premium Sales Department at (800) 221-7945 ext. 5442 or by email at MacmillanSpecialMarkets@macmillan.com.

Library of Congress Control Number: 2018945046

ISBN 978-1-250-16871-9 (hardcover) / ISBN 978-1-250-16870-2 (ebook)

Book design by Liz Dresner

First edition, 2019

10 9 8 7 6 5 4 3 2 1

swoonreads.com

For Brad:

you're my favorite

Match Me If You Can

one

Honestly, high school was stressful enough. Now I was supposed to worry about good grades *and* finding a date to homecoming? That kind of pressure just wasn't fair. I mean, talk about a major anxiety attack just waiting to happen.

Luckily for me, my best friend, Robyn, was notoriously good at matchmaking. And she was going to help me, even if I had to blackmail her with photos from our fourth-grade talent show to get it.

Because homecoming was in two weeks, and I needed a date, stat.

"What about him?" I asked, pointing toward a guy on the debate team. First period started in five minutes, and we were sitting against our lockers, scouting out potential dates in the hallway. Well, I was scouting. Robyn was ignoring me. Homeroom was over, and there wasn't much time to chat between classes. Usually I liked to be early, but desperate times called for desperate measures, and I was nothing if not desperate. "Hello?" I snapped my fingers.

Robyn sent me an annoyed look over the top of her phone.

"He's been dating a girl on the swim team for the last three months," she said, returning her focus to her phone. I leaned over to get a closer look, but she placed the phone against her chest. "Nice try."

"Another matchmaking application?" I said. Given her reaction, that was pretty much the only thing it could be. She protected the privacy of her clients like an overly aggressive goalie guarded his net.

She patted me on the head. "You're so smart. No wonder you're on the honor roll."

Robyn's matchmaking business was incredibly successful, hence her Cupid nickname. If someone wanted to utilize her mad matchmaking powers, they slid ten bucks into her locker and submitted a detailed personality test online that went to her email. After that, there was only one rule: They had to really try. When Robyn emailed them their match, they couldn't look at the name and say "pass" without going on at least one date. They had to give it their all, too, like 100 percent try their best to make it work. And honestly, with Robyn's girl-next-door looks and brown Bambi eyes, it was hard not to trust her.

Usually, things lasted a lot longer than one date, which was something she was immensely proud of. The more her couples worked, the more people were willing to go all in. Of course, then more couples worked, so it was like a never-ending cycle of matchmaking bliss. At this point, most people submitting applications took her word as fact, believing they were soul mates even if they'd never met. Given her matchmaking fame, Robyn would save up for her car in no time.

Robyn pretended like it didn't matter. But having her own car would mean freedom—she could escape whenever she needed to. Ever since they'd had the twins, it was like her parents forgot Robyn existed. She spent more time at my house than at her own, but she always had to borrow a car to come over. And ever since her dad took on some extra shifts, that had been getting trickier.

"Hey, what'd I miss?" Elena dropped her bag and sat between us, adjusting her skirt so it was merely revealing, rather than outright shocking. She'd moved into my neighborhood two years ago and was already ten times more popular than I'd ever be. But she still spent time with us mere mortals, even if she did typically eat lunch with the pretty people.

"Just talking about homecoming and how I don't have a date," I said. "So nothing new there."

She leaned her head against the lockers and heaved an exaggerated sigh. "You and me both. Man, I'm so tired I could literally fall asleep standing up. Last night I stayed up late memorizing lines for auditions, and now I can barely move."

None of us had homeroom together, so this short stretch between classes was one of the few chances we could meet up in the morning.

"Too bad. We've got a test in chemistry today," I said. Already the halls were clearing out, with students hurrying to class. I stood up. "You coming?"

"I didn't study." Elena grimaced. She looked around, as if an answer key might fall from the sky. When that didn't immediately happen, her eyes grew more furtive, darting back and forth like a caged rabbit. Then an idea seemed to hit her and an impish grin spread across her face.

Whatever she was about to do, it was probably a bad idea. I knew it, Robyn knew it, and the freshman a few feet down most likely knew it, too. But there was no stopping Elena once she put her mind to something.

Robyn stood up and we shared an uneasy look.

"Elena, what are you thinking?" I asked.

Elena got up also and leaned casually against the lockers, all traces of her earlier desperation gone. "I'm thinking we really shouldn't be cooped up inside on a beautiful October day like this."

It was only then that I noticed the fire alarm mounted on the wall next to us and how Elena was eyeing it like she would the sales rack at Nordstrom.

"You can't be serious." I stepped forward and put my hand over the plastic cover, shielding the alarm with my body. "Is that how a student council member should act?" I didn't think she'd actually do it, but I'd once watched her kiss a complete stranger on a dare, so really, I couldn't be sure. "Besides, isn't that, like, a felony or something?"

"You know, just because you're in drama doesn't mean you

need to create it," Robyn added. They were friends—90 percent of the time—but mostly by extension. Sometimes Robyn found Elena's attitude a little . . . over the top.

Elena pantomimed looking wounded, throwing her straight black hair over one shoulder and placing her hands over her heart. "I do *not* create drama."

Then she shoved me out of the way, opened the alarm's clear cover, and pushed down on the white lever inside before Robyn or I could stop her. It happened so fast, I barely had time to regain my balance. Then it was too late.

Sirens blared overhead, annoyingly loud to the point where I felt like my ears would bleed from the sheer volume. It was impossible to think, which was ironically counter-productive to the sirens' whole purpose.

"What did you just do?" I yelled, clamping my hands over my ears.

"I didn't think it'd actually work," she yelled back, her eyes growing wide. A lot of times Elena's expressions were comi-cally theatrical—I blamed her interest in acting—but one look at her face and I knew her surprise was genuine.

"Like they'd be props or something?" Robyn threw her hands in the air. "Honestly, I'm going to match you up with a rock for homecoming." She grabbed Elena's bag off the floor as I pushed us all down the hallway—away from the scene of the crime.

"I don't know, everything else in this school is so old . . . I mean, we don't even have security cameras here."

Before she'd moved to Oregon, Elena had gone to a much

larger, more technologically advanced school in California—one that had better computers, HD televisions in every room, and lightning-fast internet. Right now, though, I bet she was glad our tiny school didn't have all the cameras and security that she was used to. We only had a few cameras at the main entrances, and every student knew how to get around them.

Elena looked back over her shoulder, then to the left and right, where a crowd of students streamed down the hallway toward the doors.

It was surreal. I'd been through fire drills before but had never experienced the gut-wrenching nervousness that I'd soon see my head—or diploma—on the chopping block.

Other students laughed as they walked through the doors leading to the parking lot. I sweated. A lot. Maybe it'd be a good thing if the sprinklers went off. At least that way, my sweaty armpits wouldn't be so noticeable.

The sirens weren't as loud outside, but my pulse still beat overtime. Students milled around the flagpole, down the sidewalk, and in between all the cars. My goal was to go as far back as possible. Maybe that would help our chances of going undetected.

But we didn't make it that far.

"Hold up, Mia." Principal Egeus seemed to appear out of nowhere, his signature stern look in full force. He had ex–Navy SEAL written all over him. I wasn't sure if he had actually been a Navy SEAL, but with his height and weight, he could have been. "A student informed me that you or

Elena might know something about"—he waved his arm in the air, encompassing all the noise and cacophony around us—"this."

My mind had chosen the absolute worst moment to go blank, but for the life of me, I couldn't come up with a single coherent sentence. I'd been busted, and now I was done for. Goodbye journalism program at NYU; it'd been a nice thought while it lasted. Elena was supposed to be good at improv, but even she seemed at a loss for words. She'd probably be kicked off student council and could see her prom-planning leverage disappearing before her eyes.

"They were in the library with me."

It was the voice of an angel, coming at the perfect moment to save me from Principal Egeus's withering stare. But it wasn't Robyn, like I'd been expecting. She was standing next to me, looking as panicked as I felt. No, the voice had been distinctly male. I turned around to see my savior and was surprised to find Vince Demetrius, our school's golden boy and probably the one person alive who might be able to convince the principal that we were clear of any wrongdoing. He was one of Elena's best friends and the star athlete of our high school's soccer team. Everyone loved him.

Everyone including, I was hoping, the principal.

"Elena needed someone to run lines with her for the auditions tonight, so I read one part and Mia read the other." Vince flashed a smile, and I melted into a puddle. I was so grateful, I could have kissed him right then and there. Then again, that urge was nothing new.

Principal Egeus nodded once before swiping a hand over his face. "All right, the student probably saw someone else."

I bobbed my head like this was a distinct possibility. After all, I had fairly average looks. My brown hair was usually in loose waves around my face, and my eyes were kind of a murky blue; nothing noteworthy there. Elena, on the other hand . . . well, with her Hollywood looks and gorgeous skin, there was no way anyone would mistake her for anyone else, except maybe a young Vanessa Hudgens. Still, the principal nodded again, like that sealed the deal.

"Well, we should have this all sorted out soon so you can return to class," he said. "Be sure to check in with your first-period teacher so everyone's accounted for."

Then he was gone, and I was floating.

"Vince, that was amazing!" Elena threw her arms around his neck. "Are you sure you won't audition for the show with me? You're a natural."

Vince shrugged his broad shoulders and released Elena, stepping back somewhat awkwardly. "My place is on a soccer field, not a stage."

"You seriously saved us back there," I said. The euphoria was making me giddy and impulsive, and without thinking about it, I reached up and placed a quick peck on his cheek. Of course, the second my heels came back down on the pavement, embarrassment caught up with me. I mean, we were somewhat friends through Elena, but really, Vince was way out of my league. He took it in stride, though, acting like that sort of thing happened all the time. And maybe it did.

"Hey, Robyn," he said, giving her a nod. "Good job matching Shawn and Jaden together. They're like a couple of octopuses. Octopi? Whatever. Guess you were right."

"I was right about your friend Justin, too," she said, looking smug. "He and Tara are so cute together, I can't stand it."

Vince shook his head. "Yeah, they're pretty sickening, too."

It was obvious from his smile that he approved. And with two of his friends happily matched, it was only a matter of time before he requested Robyn's services—if he hadn't already.

An idea began to take shape in my mind, and I looked over at Robyn.

Elena shrugged, probably bored with the conversation, and hooked her arm through Vince's.

"Okay, well, I can't make a liar out of you, so now you need to run lines with me," Elena said. "You don't have a choice." She began to pull him away. "With any luck, I'll have all period to rehearse."

Elena had one superpower, and that was how easily she could give everyone around her emotional whiplash. It was like she had zero memory of pulling the fire alarm and felt no guilt for behaving so recklessly. It was both her curse and part of her charm—Elena lived life loud and took no prisoners. Two fire trucks pulled up to the front of the high school, but Elena had already moved on.

"She seems really upset about all this," Robyn mused, twirling a strand of her blond hair around her pointer finger. "Think we should send her a gift basket?"

That was such a typical Robyn comment. Elena kept us spontaneous, Robyn brought the laughter, and I made sure we made it out alive.

I liked having a plan. A plan for what, who knew? The zombie apocalypse? Armageddon? It didn't matter. I liked knowing what was going to happen next. And what would happen next for several weeks and even years.

And the next item on my agenda was finding a date. Maybe Robyn hoped I'd let the matter drop. But she knew me well enough to know that was never going to happen.

"Forget about Elena," I said, my earlier idea blossoming in my mind. "I know who you should match me up with for homecoming."

Robyn raised her eyebrows but otherwise didn't comment.

"Vince," I said. I mean, Vince was the star soccer player and runner-up for homecoming king. He had blond boy-band hair that always looked amazing in pictures and a great physique that would fill out a suit perfectly. And if Robyn matched us up, I might actually have a shot.

She scrunched her eyes and looked off in the distance, like somehow the answer was there among the crowd of students mingling around us.

"Yeah, I'm not seeing it," she said finally. "Sorry."

She didn't *look* sorry.

"Come on," I said. "We have so many things in common." I began ticking the items off on my fingers. "We're both kind of overachievers in our own way, him with soccer and me with journalism. He even reads the school newspaper—I've seen him. We care about our grades, and he's the responsible type of guy who doesn't party every night, even though he could. It makes all kinds of logical sense. The only question is, has he filled out one of your applications?"

I knew Robyn wouldn't answer me outright about Vince's application, but her silence spoke volumes. She looked away and began picking at her nails.

"You don't need another overachiever who can pencil you in on the weekends," she said. "You don't even really know him. You just like the *idea* of him. And you can't logically decide who your best match is supposed to be. There's a reason why they call it a matter of the heart, Mia. Have you ever heard that opposites attract? You'd be better with someone who's more laid-back."

"You mean, you want me to settle." I crossed my arms. "You think I couldn't possibly interest someone like him."

She shook her head. "That's not what I'm saying. Look, you don't make sense with Vince," she said, glancing around before lowering her voice. "Besides, you're going to fall hard for someone else pretty soon. I know it. Believe me, I've seen your results."

I had filled out one of her personality tests, just for fun. Robyn kept threatening to set me up on a date, and I'd never taken her up on it. Of course, now when I really wanted her to, she was being a brat.

"Who is it?" I asked. "What percentage was our match on your personality test?"

"I mean, I've seen *your* results and I know you. Logan

hasn't filled one out, but he's been flirting hard practically all year. Sure, he started out kind of subtle, but he's been laying it on pretty thick lately. You can't pretend like you haven't noticed."

Oh. No. She. *Didn't*.

"Logan?" I put as much scorn into the name as I could without drawing the attention of anyone around me. "You can't possibly mean the same Logan who once put bubble gum in my hair and wore the same Batman T-shirt every day for an entire year. The same Logan who never takes anything seriously and teases me daily. That Logan?"

"He's *flirting* with you, Mia. And the Batman shirt thing was in the second grade. Just think about it."

Then she had the audacity to wink.

Yeah, that was *so* not happening.

two

I had detention during lunch, but not for my involvement with the fire alarm. I'd dodged that bullet, only to be busted for something so much less incriminating.

To be honest, I was kind of proud of myself. Detention was a new experience for me, like a rite of passage. True, it'd be a different story if I actually deserved it, or if it went on my permanent record. The fire alarm still haunted my thoughts with its screeching accusation. But detention with my best friend? For an infraction so minor even my mom would find it funny? That didn't seem so bad.

I pushed open the door, Robyn close behind me. I handed our slip to Mr. Cho at the front of the room, who eyed it lazily.

"You're both in detention because you were disrespectful to a teacher?" he asked.

Robyn snorted. "Mrs. Patterson kept calling Africa a country, and Mia corrected her in front of the class. I backed her up, because hello, it's a continent. Mrs. Patterson got defensive. How is that our fault?"

Mr. Cho's lip quivered like he was holding back a laugh. He motioned for us to take a seat but otherwise didn't give us any instructions on how we were to spend our time, so we pulled out our lunches. It made no difference to me whether we ate here or in the cafeteria, as long as I had time to convince Robyn to set me up with Vince. Homecoming was only two weeks away. Time was running out before he found another date.

"So about Vince," I said.

Robyn sighed. "Okay," she said. "I know that nothing I say is going to convince you. So I'm giving you some homework."

I set my drink on the table. "I think I've got enough of that already, thank you very much."

She kept talking like I'd never even said anything.

"You say you like logic, yeah? So write a pros-and-cons list." She pointed a finger at me. "Compare Vince and Logan. You know I'm right; you just need to see it."

Fat chance. But I'd do it to appease her. I picked up my sandwich and took a big bite.

But then Logan walked in and I stopped mid-chew.

Had Logan gotten detention simply so he could taunt me some more? That would be just like him. Or maybe Robyn had tipped him off, believing herself to be "helping." That would be just like her, too. I glanced at my friend, accusation written on my face. But she held up her hands in the universal *it wasn't me* gesture, and I guessed I believed her. Logan probably had detention a lot—he wasn't exactly known for being a great student. Yet another reason why we were total opposites and Robyn was way off in thinking we'd be a good match. And something for Logan's con list.

Logan handed his slip to Mr. Cho, who read it and frowned.

"You were late, again?"

Logan nodded once, causing his shaggy hair to fall into his eyes. He brushed it aside with a hand, saw me, and grinned.

Mr. Cho sighed. "Have a seat."

Logan pulled up a chair, situating himself to my left, across from Robyn. His arm brushed mine, and I pretended not to notice.

"Let me guess," Logan said. "You got detention for"—he pursed his lips as if he were deep in thought—"dog-earing a page in a library book."

I shook my head but didn't say anything. My reason for being here actually wasn't much worse than that. Which meant I was all kinds of lame, even if I'd been proud of getting detention earlier. I really needed to get a life.

He leaned back in his chair and studied me. "No hints? Okay, did you finish an assignment early and read a book when you were supposed to be working?"

It was kind of scary how well Logan knew me, which was probably how he could push my buttons so easily.

I shook my head and took another bite of my sandwich. Robyn was watching this whole exchange with entirely too much interest, so I kicked her under the table. She didn't even flinch; she just smirked.

Logan raised his eyebrows and leaned forward on an elbow. "You mean you actually did something . . . wrong?" He shook his head.

"She corrected a teacher," Robyn said, throwing a potato chip at my head. "Shocking, I know."

Logan laughed, and I resisted the urge to kick Robyn again.

"Well, what about you, Mr. Hotshot?" I asked him. "Why were you late?"

He lowered his voice and whispered dramatically, "Wouldn't you like to know?"

This caused goose bumps to rise along my arms, but I ignored the sensation. Logan was up to his usual tricks again, and it got to me. Robyn might call it flirting, but I knew it for what it really was. Logan simply liked his games, and I was an easy target. I'd never seen Logan *not* behave like this toward me—which made it that much more difficult to believe he was acting out of any secret feelings he harbored. Who liked one person for that long?

I inspected the person beside me, curious as to why my best friend would think we were a good match. Sure, he was good-looking, I guess, if you were into that artsy creative look (which I wasn't). He had dimples (which, okay, were kind of cute), but he also had messy brown hair that hung over his eyes (which made him look like he had just rolled out of bed—*so* not my style). His olive skin gave off the impression of a year-round tan, which I'd always been jealous of (not that I'd ever admit it).

He had a tall and lean frame, but that wasn't what I typically went for in guys. At all. Robyn knew that. I usually liked them muscular like Vince, whose chiseled abs could shred cheese. I'd give him one thing. Logan did have nice eyes. They were kind of a chocolate color, with lighter specks in them. Not that I was looking at his eyes or anything.

I startled when someone knocked on the classroom window. Elena and Vince peered through the glass, their faces distorted in the old pane.

As one, Logan, Robyn, and I looked at Mr. Cho to see his reaction. Mr. Cho glanced up, shrugged, and went back to reading *Better Homes and Gardens*.

Before he could change his mind, I jumped up from my seat and went to the window, cracking it open.

"What are you guys doing here?" I asked them, pushing against the window to see if it would open any farther.

"Providing sustenance," Vince said, passing two ice-cream sandwiches through the frame. "Sorry, man," he called to Logan. "Didn't know you were in here, too, or we'd have brought more."

I clutched the sandwiches to my chest, forgetting momentarily that this was probably not the best course of action for frozen treats. Looking over at Robyn, I tried to telepathically make her recognize the better match here. I mean, nice boy who rescued me from the principal, bought me ice cream, and had an amazing soccer body, or trouble boy who landed in detention and probably wouldn't want to go to homecoming even if it meant supporting a school event? It was an easy decision, one that Vince won hands-down.

But either my best-friend telepathy wasn't working, or Robyn chose to ignore it. She popped a potato chip in her mouth and crunched it loudly.

"I'm good," she said. "Logan can have mine." But Logan shook his head, too, so I was left holding two slightly squishy ice-cream sandwiches.

"And we came to bust you out of here," Elena said, stretching up on her toes to better lean in through the window frame. "Come on, Mr. Cho, you know they aren't hardened criminals. What do you say?"

Elena did her best innocent pout, the expression she'd perfected so much that it would one day be her ticket to Hollywood.

Mr. Cho pursed his lips. Eventually he sighed, placed his magazine on the desk, and stood up. The thrill of victory coursed through my veins.

"I don't want to be here, either. All of you go enjoy the rest of lunch," he said, glancing between the three of us. "But I get the extra ice-cream sandwich."

He was releasing Logan also. But why? If anyone deserved to be here, it was Logan for repeatedly being late.

I guessed it didn't really matter. I still got out of detention. Plus, I'd gotten a free ice-cream sandwich out of the deal, which was a bonus. I'd experienced my rite of passage and was now free to crush on the beautiful boy bearing gifts. It was a win-win in my book. Of course, now that we'd be hanging out with Vince, I couldn't exactly talk to Robyn about him. I'd have to find another time to convince her to set us up. It wasn't like I'd forget about it, and the clock was ticking.

Robyn scowled at me as she picked up her lunch—maybe she'd finally caught on to my telepathy—but it lacked any real sting. I handed the extra ice-cream sandwich off to Mr. Cho and tore open the wrapper on mine, taking a celebratory bite.

Logan hadn't unpacked anything, so he simply grabbed his bag from off the floor and slung it over one shoulder.

"Catch you later," he said as he passed me. "Might even be sooner than you think."

Then he walked away, not looking back.

three

The weekend was calling my name. I just had to get through journalism first. After the excitement of detention, the rest of my day had been tedious, and I was looking forward to vegging out in front of Netflix all night. I walked through the classroom door and stopped dead in my tracks. Elena bumped into me from behind.

"What's he doing here?" I asked, nodding in the direction of the back corner.

"Logan?" Elena said. "I don't know. It's a little late in the year to change schedules."

So this was what Logan had been hinting at. I smelled a fish, and that fish had Robyn's name written all over it. Sure, she supposedly didn't set people up without their permission, but there's a first time for everything.

I didn't say anything else as I navigated my way to my

seat and opened my notebook. Elena plopped her books on the table next to me, and together we stared at the person who dared intrude on our happy journalism family.

Robyn swept in at the last minute, claiming the seat to my left and dropping her books on the table with a loud thump. This was one reason journalism was my favorite class—it was the only one Robyn, Elena, and I had together.

"All right, everybody, listen up!" Mr. Quince called from the front of the classroom. "I'd like you all to welcome Logan to the team. He'll be the new photographer for the *Athens High Herald*."

From where he stood, leaning against the wall, Logan gave a small wave in acknowledgment. Did he even *read* the paper?

"Spencer bit off more than he could chew with his AP classes, so he had to leave our staff. You guys have no idea how hard it was to find a photographer who also had a free eighth period, so please be nice to him."

Well, that explained a few things. But Spencer wasn't just the photographer—he also wrote for the sports section. I wondered who Mr. Quince would bully into taking on an additional article. Our teacher stood impatiently at the front of the class, his eyebrows raised in a silent question. "Well, any takers on the sports column?"

I pictured Vince in his soccer shorts, and I couldn't help but smile in appreciation.

"I like sports, sir," I said, raising my hand.

He didn't hesitate. "Good. You'll cover Spencer's column. There's a game tomorrow night. Don't miss it."

He cleared his throat. "Now for a bit of bad news," Mr. Quince said. "Or good, if you're a glass-half-full kind of person. But circulation has been somewhat down this year, and the school is debating whether the cost of running a high school paper is worth it. They're considering getting rid of the paper or drastically cutting down on the number of issues. Most of our readers are online, which doesn't cost to print, but cutting back would mean they wouldn't have to pay me as much for formatting and editing, and the funds could go toward the football team."

I wondered how this could possibly be considered good news, and judging from the confused looks going on around me, I wasn't the only one. If they shut down the paper, Mr. Quince would still have a job as our teacher, but I already knew the journalism basics he taught at the beginning of each class. I took this course for the real-life paper experience. I was counting on the fact that college newspapers looked for that kind of thing. And the sporadic class assignments Mr. Quince handed out unrelated to the paper weren't enough to get me that.

"I need your creativity now more than ever. Please let me know if you have any ideas on how to increase readership of our paper or ways to convince the administration of the efficacy of our program. I'm working on creating a contest and will let you know when I have more details. For now, keep up the good work."

Mr. Quince clapped his hands twice. "No lesson today. Work on the inverted pyramid method in your next pieces. The next paper goes to bed by eleven on Saturday, so don't dawdle, people." Everyone went back to their individual projects, looking unfazed. Except for me. Without the high school paper, could I still get scholarships? How could I get on a college paper without experience? And how come no one was acting nearly as concerned as I felt?

Joey drummed his fingers on the table as he walked by. "Now you're doing sports?" he asked me. Everything was a joke to him, which was appropriate, since he drew the comics for the newspaper. "I know you love journalism and all, but you don't even like sports."

"Plus you already write an opinion piece and do the daily videos for school announcements," Robyn added. She liked to take Joey's side, no matter what argument he was making. I blamed his green eyes. Robyn had a thing for those.

I slumped back in my chair.

"Well, it's not like the video announcements really count as reporting," I said. Sure, they got me comfortable in front of a camera, but I didn't want to be a television reporter. I wanted to be a journalist, writing the news stories that really mattered. I couldn't tell them I'd volunteered only so I could see Vince play, though. It was too embarrassing.

Joey left and Robyn watched him go. Logan came over to where we sat. He pulled a chair from a nearby table and sat on it backward, his arms folded across the back as he smiled at me.

"So," he said, drawing out the word.

"So?" I repeated. I refused to look over at Robyn. She was so off base in thinking Logan flirted with me. *Taunted* sounded more accurate to me.

"It looks like you'll be covering the soccer game tomorrow night."

"Looks like it."

He pulled a black gel pen out of his pocket. I barely had time to register surprise when he reached across the table, took my hand, and started writing on my palm.

"Hey! What do you think you're doing?" I asked, trying to pull my arm away.

"Careful, you don't want to mess it up," he said, holding tight. The pen tickled my palm and I tried not to laugh. After all, I was supposed to be angry, and laughing kind of spoiled the effect.

"You done yet?" I asked.

In answer, he let go of my wrist and capped the pen. My hand tingled where he had held it, and I quickly pulled it back, inspecting his work. His name and phone number covered my palm. Well, that was just great.

"Is this your weird way of asking me out?" I asked, staring at my hand. I was so going to chew Robyn out for this later. She'd probably told him to up his game. Robyn busied herself to my left, flipping between notebooks like she wasn't paying attention to us at all.

"No. Is that your way of saying you want me to?"

Logan smirked, and I balled up my other hand into a fist,

but he pulled away before I could hit his shoulder. He held up his hands in surrender.

"We'll have to work together on your sports piece. You can call me to let me know what shots you'll need."

"Couldn't you just email me some standard soccer pictures from the game?" I said. "You know, players kicking the ball and stuff."

"Where's the fun in that?" he asked. Then he stood up with a smirk, pushed his chair back under the table, and walked away.

I still refused to look at Robyn. Instead I glanced over at Elena, who was watching me with one eyebrow raised.

"What?" I asked, daring her to comment.

"I think someone likes you," she said in a singsong voice. Robyn laughed and tried to turn it into a cough.

"And I think the whiteboard-marker fumes are going to your head," I said. "We have to work together for the article, that's all."

I was doing damage control, because Elena ran the gossip column. Since she was on student council, she knew a lot of the issues going on around the school. Plus drama and gossip kind of came hand in hand, so it made sense. I didn't need her starting any rumors and ruining my chances with Vince, though. Logically, he was still my best bet for homecoming.

Logan and I were more likely to be voted "polar opposites" in the school yearbook than "cutest couple." Even if we survived the dance, it could never go anywhere after that.

Besides, I didn't need a slacker date who'd show up late with bedhead, which seemed like something Logan would do. If he went to the dance at all. It'd be best to ignore him altogether.

"Uh-huh," Elena said. "Then why don't I see him giving his number to anyone else?"

"Told you so," Robyn said. Even the way she flipped through her notebook looked smug.

"You're delusional," I said to them both. They let the conversation drop, but occasionally I'd see Elena making kissy faces at me and looking pointedly in Logan's direction. It was like she wanted to stir up trouble, which, now that I thought about it, was pretty typical.

Robyn worked on her Dear Robyn column while I plotted ways to kill her in her sleep. If she'd convinced Logan to pull that stunt with the gel pen, I'd put those fourth-grade talent-show pictures in next week's paper. Who knew, maybe it'd help with newspaper circulation and solve the problem of discontinuing our paper.

Most everyone was busy working on their articles for tomorrow's deadline—in addition to the other weekly nights, Mr. Quince came in on Saturdays to submit the next issue to the printer—but I'd already finished my opinion piece. So, I used my class time as productively as possible (doodling in my notebook and planning what dress would best match Vince's eyes). The more I thought about the prospect of homecoming with Vince, the more excited I got.

A few minutes minutes before class ended, I heard Mr. Quince call my name.

"Mia, don't you have to leave for announcements?"

I jerked my head from my hand and stood up so fast, my chair fell over. I was late. The last five minutes of each school day were reserved for school announcements, and it would take me a while to make it to the office. Tania, the girl who did them with me, was probably breathing into a brown paper bag by now. I grabbed my books and ran out of the room.

A teacher in the hall gave me an odd look as I tore past, my shoes slapping against the linoleum. At least I'd worn flats. I rounded the corner and hurtled into the office, nearly bowling over the receptionist.

"I know, I know, I'm sorry," I said, out of breath. "Let's go."

I slid into my chair, barely glancing at Tania, who was fidgeting with the papers on the desk in front of us. The scowling receptionist hit the button on the recorder, and we were live to more than a hundred classrooms in Athens High.

Tania did a double take when she looked at me, no doubt because I'd run harder in the last few minutes than I had in a whole month of gym. I wasn't exactly the athletic type. My face was probably red enough to be mistaken for a fire hydrant.

Tania's eyes were wide as she looked back at the live camera. She slid the papers over to me, trying to catch my eye, but I couldn't let her capture my attention when I needed to focus on the announcements. I glanced through the papers as she started talking about the north parking lot and how it was reserved for seniors only. By the time she got to the plea for people to stop putting their gum under the desks, I had placed the papers to the side.

"So please stop being gross," she said, and turned to me.

I plastered on my hundred-kilowatt smile and addressed the camera.

"The firefighters have determined that the alarm this morning was a prank or accident, and there's nothing to worry about there." I managed to keep a straight face and barreled right on to the next announcement without blinking an eye. Go me. "The varsity soccer team is playing the Jordan Knights tomorrow at seven, so bring your school spirit and support your Lions," I said. "Don't forget that the concessions stand only takes cash, so come prepared. Other than that, have a great weekend, and don't do anything stupid."

Tania and I smiled at the camera in silence. This was always the awkward part—waiting for the receptionist to turn the camera off. After five beats of silence, Tania turned to me.

"So do you have a crush on Logan or what?" she asked.

"What? No!" Robyn. Was. Dead. Meat. She was spreading rumors about us? Sure, he'd been kind of flirty. Maybe? But that was just who he was—a tease. I could tell Tania didn't believe me, so I scrambled for anything that might get her off my back. "I have a thing for Vince, not Logan. Jeez, what gave you that idea?"

She pointed to my face.

"You have Logan's name and phone number written across

your cheek. It's backward, though, so it took me a second to figure it out."

My eyes widened and my hand flew to my face—the same hand that Logan had written on earlier. It didn't take a genius to figure out that I had rested my head on my hand and the ink had transferred.

I gasped. "Why didn't you tell me? Give me a mirror."

"Because you were late and we started as soon as you ran in here," she said, handing me a small compact.

I flipped it open and groaned when I saw my reflection. "It was like this the whole time?" I asked. "That's so embarrassing." My chances with Vince were rapidly dwindling. Now Robyn would *have* to step in. I tried rubbing at the ink, but that did nothing. Who knew gel pens were this stubborn?

"Ummm . . . ladies?" The receptionist cleared her throat.

"Can't you see I'm in the middle of a crisis?" I asked. I pulled at my cheeks and made a hideous face in the mirror. I looked like a circus freak.

"Ladies . . . the recorder is still on. You're live."

That got my attention. My eyes flew to the recorder, where the blinking red light seemed to mock my mortification.

"What?" It came out as a squeak.

"I'm sorry, the button was stuck . . ." Her voice trailed off, and she shrugged in apology.

"Ummm . . ." My voice was wobbly, so I tried to sound confident. "It's okay, we were practicing a skit. Yes, everyone please come to the soccer game, where you can all paint your faces, but remember not to use pens . . ."

The receptionist pushed the button hard, and the light turned off.

"Mia, stop hyperventilating," Tania said. I whipped around to face her. "Wow, your eyes are really wide. It's okay, just calm down."

"Calm down?" I said. "Calm down?" My voice was too high, too nervous. "I just announced to the entire school that I have a crush on Vince, and, as if that weren't enough, my face looks like *this*!" I jabbed a finger at my cheek and held it there for emphasis. Tania reached out and pulled my shaking hand back to my lap.

"People will forget all about it over the weekend."

I didn't bother correcting her. This was high school. She should know better. No one forgot anything. Ever.

I put my head on the table and covered it with my arms. Tania patted my back awkwardly, like I was a dog she suspected had fleas. Then she picked up her bag and left me to my misery.

My thoughts were darker than the pen scrawled across my palm (and, lest I forget, my face). There was no way I'd live this down. I'd be the brunt of every joke, the laughing-stock of the junior class. And I could kiss homecoming good-bye, especially with someone like Vince. I banged my head against the table a few times before giving up. It was hopeless. Nothing could save me now.

I'd just committed social suicide.

four

I pulled a Moaning Myrtle and hid out in a bathroom stall for the next half hour, waiting for people to clear the halls. It was the only safe place. On my way from the office, everyone had laughed at me, and that wasn't an exaggeration. It was like a wave—one that only got louder as people stopped to stare. On the plus side, at least they weren't talking about me behind my back. On the downside, it was only because they were too busy laughing at my face.

One girl I didn't recognize said "I feel so bad for her," and I almost tackle-hugged her out of gratitude. But that was before she finished her statement with "Vince is obviously way out of her league."

Now, safely sequestered in a bathroom, I occasionally heard girls come and go, but after a while, the noise dwindled down.

To top it all off, I'd gotten my entire shirt wet when I tried to stick the side of my face under the faucet. Go me.

My phone dinged with a text message from Robyn.

—How're you holding up? Wanna get ice cream?

Yes, I did, but eating my feelings wouldn't solve my problems. Maybe I'd feel better if Vince asked me to homecoming. At least then people would stop gossiping about me.

There in the Athens High girls' bathroom, time seemed to slow down. This actually could be the answer to my problems. The thought lodged in my brain and strangled out all common sense. If Vince asked me out, it wouldn't matter that I had announced my crush to the school. It wouldn't matter that I'd had Logan's name scrawled across my cheek. It wouldn't matter, because I'd be dating the most popular guy in the junior class.

Once I'd thought of it, I couldn't ignore it. The thought of facing everyone made me want to shrivel up and die, but if I could change things, well, that was another story. I texted Robyn back.

—No ice cream. But now you have to match me with Vince. It's the only way to save face. Please, please, please.

Her response was immediate.

—Save face? I didn't think you'd be ready to make puns about this yet. ;)

I scowled at my phone, even though she couldn't see it, and responded.

—Not. Helping.

I tried to wait patiently for her to text me back but couldn't stop myself from nervously tapping on the sink.

—You know I love you, but no can do. It wouldn't be fair to him. Plus that would give me loads of bad business karma. Don't worry, I'll get things worked out with your homecoming date soon.

Yeah. That was what I was worried about. And if Robyn was going to keep pushing Logan on me, I needed to act fast.

A janitor came into the bathroom and gave me a sympathetic smile that made me want to curl up in the fetal position. If a grown-up felt sorry for me, I really was officially at the bottom of the social ladder. I put my phone away and tried to act normal, but there was no normal for this situation.

"Have you tried using hand sanitizer?" the janitor asked. "That's what I used on my three-year-old when she got into the markers."

I wanted to laugh, but the comparison also made me want

to cry. Instead I just mumbled "Thanks" and pretended to be invisible. The janitor took the hint, checked off the paper that said the bathrooms were clean enough, and left without another word. I eyed the hand-sanitizer dispenser that was mounted on the wall and squared my shoulders. I was going to get this pen off my face and then I was going to take charge of my life by matching myself with Vince. I knew how Robyn's matchmaking business worked, and I knew how she emailed results back to her clients. All I needed to do was log on to her email and seal the deal.

My stomach squeezed uncomfortably at the thought of going behind my best friend's back, but I chose to ignore it. I also chose to ignore what Robyn had said about Logan, because right now, I needed concrete solutions, not crazy theories.

Robyn was forcing my hand. Friendship should come before work. Besides, it was one measly date—what could possibly go wrong?

"All right, let's see what you can do," I said to the hand sanitizer. Then I started pumping.

It did the trick. My cheek was red from all the rubbing, but it was better than the alternative. I could show my face in public again. Now I just needed a game plan. If I logged in from my phone, Robyn might get an alert of suspicious behavior on her account. I needed to log in from a device she typically used. I could go to her house, but she'd ask too many questions. No, I needed somewhere close.

Somewhere like the computer lab.

I picked up my bag and made my way there, all the while trying to look inconspicuous but failing miserably. Being bad was a whole lot more stressful than it looked. I practically sweated guilt as I walked down the hall.

Luckily, there weren't many people around to see. The few students who were still there gave silent smirks, but I ignored them.

I peeked around the corner of the computer lab and watched the teacher, Ms. Lackey, through the door. She checked her watch and closed the lid of her laptop, sliding it into her bag before standing up. I'd hidden out in the bathroom for so long that even the teachers were leaving. She turned off the light, closed the door, and locked it before heading down the hall, away from my hiding place.

Now was my chance.

As soon as she was out of sight, I rounded the corner and studied the lock. It was the cheap, run-of-the-mill kind, which meant Robyn's old trick would work.

When we were eight, Robyn went through a detective phase, reading every Nancy Drew book she could get from the library. From there, it blossomed into a full-blown obsession, with fingerprinting kits, invisible ink, secret codes, and, yes, lock picking. I'd been relieved when she moved on to other interests, but now I was glad for the knowledge I'd gleaned from her.

I dropped my bag on the floor and rooted through it until I found my student ID. Then I wiggled the card in between the lock and doorframe, smiling when the door swung open.

It was almost too easy. Of course, getting caught would put a damper on things, so I stepped inside and quietly closed the door behind me, leaving the lights off.

I went to the corner Robyn liked and powered the computer on, nervously tapping my fingers on the desk. I couldn't help but glance at the door every other minute to make sure no one saw me. At this rate, I'd have a crick in my neck before I even got to the main screen.

After what seemed like a decade and a half, the lock screen came up and prompted me for a password. I used Robyn's and waited while the computer logged me—I mean her—on.

I was chewing my lips so much, I'd need a pound of lip balm to undo all the damage. Picturing Robyn's face made me physically nauseous. But this was the only option. Gossip grows the longer it goes unchecked, and I didn't need people talking about me several years from now at our high school reunion.

Before I could talk myself out of it, I opened her email and found Vince's matchmaking application. I clicked REPLY and copied over the template she used whenever she responded to clients. Then I wrote my name on the blank line. The cursor blinked again and again, silently accusing me with every heartbeat.

Of course, a regular date with Vince might not make everyone forget about my little performance from earlier. It'd have to be something big. I hadn't considered it before, but most students probably wouldn't even know if we went out one time, and Robyn's contract only required one date. I added a line at the end of Robyn's template. *I think homecoming would be a great place to start*, I wrote. Then I took a deep breath, the cursor hovering over the SEND button.

I could feel my heartbeat slow down with the knowledge that soon everything would go back to normal. Plus, I'd have a hot date to homecoming.

I jumped when someone behind me cleared their throat. Instinctively, my hands clenched, my finger pressed down on the button, and the email was sent.

What had I done?

"Well, well, what do we have here? Mia Taylor breaking the rules?"

I whipped around in the chair so fast, I almost fell on the floor.

"Logan! What are you doing here?" I was mortified that he'd caught me doing something I shouldn't, but more importantly, he was seeing me with my face scrubbed raw, free of makeup, one side redder than the other, and with a wet shirt thrown in for good measure. It wasn't fair that he could stand there looking so casually cool while I looked like something the cat had thrown up. If he'd been less good-looking, maybe my ego wouldn't be as bruised, but all I could do now was pretend like it didn't bother me.

"I asked you first," he said, arms crossed over his chest. He leaned on the doorframe, the *open* doorframe, his shoulders taking up nearly the entire space.

"Research," I said.

He crossed the room to me and looked over my shoulder at the computer screen. I hastily archived Vince's email, but it was too late.

"Uh-huh. And what type of research involves stalking poor, unsuspecting guys?" His face was so close to mine, I could feel his breath on my neck.

"He's hardly unsuspecting, thanks to you," I muttered, closing the program. I logged out and pushed back from the desk. "If you absolutely must know, I needed to learn his full name and birthday . . . for the sports article I'm writing." Any minute now, Logan was going to call me out on my horrible lying skills, I knew it. But he nodded like my answer made perfect sense.

"And you couldn't just ask him? I mean, the guy's a tool, but he wouldn't give you the cold shoulder." His tone was tense, like he was holding back something else.

I raised my eyebrows. "You obviously don't like him," I said. "What's that all about?"

Logan looked away. "It's not that. He's decent enough. It's just . . . it's like we're always competing with each other, and he always gets what I want."

I waited, sensing there was more to it.

He sighed. "Back in third grade, he won a community art competition, and I came in second by one point. In eighth, he got to have a free period as a teacher's aide while I had to endure another year of PE, even though I did extracurricular sports, too. Freshman year, he won that sports essay contest and got to pick the winning mascot design for our school."

"Poor baby," I said, puckering my lips to show I was kidding. "You're still mad about him winning an art competition in third grade?"

"No," Logan said. "It's just that he keeps on doing it."

"Oh?" I smiled. "What does he have now that you want?"

Logan didn't answer. He just looked at me. I changed the subject.

"So," I said, picking up my bag and slinging it over my shoulder. "Do you have a crush on the computer-lab teacher, or is there some other reason why you're here?"

"You have quite the interest in my love life lately, don't you?" he said, and I felt my cheeks go hot. "First you think I'm asking you out, and now you think I'm into cougars?" He tsked. "You couldn't just stop at publicly embarrassing me over the announcements?"

"I didn't mean to. Honestly." Was that too apologetic? I didn't want to encourage him. What if Robyn had said something to him? About me? I cleared my throat and opted for a more formal apology. "Sorry, I didn't mean to embarrass you or reject you over the announcements or anything."

He smiled, and I fiddled with the computer mouse. Well, this was officially awkward. I stood up and tried to brush past him, but he was focusing on something else and didn't notice my attempt to leave. Because he didn't step back like I was expecting, I clumsily tried to scoot between him and the desk and had to put a hand on his chest to keep from falling over. I hastily snatched it back, but not before noticing that Logan's muscles were more defined than *Webster's Dictionary*.

"Ummm, excuse me," I said.

"I guess I'll see you at the game tomorrow?" he asked as he slid into the seat and logged on to the computer.

I hovered uncertainly by the desk, torn between wanting to get out of here as fast as I could and seeing what Logan was up to. What was he doing here after computer-lab hours? Would he rat me out to the lab teacher? Probably not, but it wouldn't hurt to be sure. Besides, I couldn't leave without knowing why he was here. It was the reporter in my blood that demanded answers.

"How'd you unlock the computer-lab door?" I asked, placing a hand on my hip. I knew for a fact it had closed behind me.

"I have a key."

"What?" I leaned in without thinking about it.

He raised his eyebrows. "Unlike you, I'm actually sup-posed to be here," he said. Then he smiled, which took the sting out of the words. I realized how close I was standing to him and took a step back. He didn't comment on it, but he was still smiling as he turned back to the computer and clicked on a file. "I'm uploading some pictures to the server so the yearbook staff can access them. There are too many to send via email, so once a week or so I upload some photos I took, and they'll sort and categorize them throughout the year."

"Don't you need to tell them who's who?" I asked.

"Nah, I'm just the photographer. Captioning the photos is their job." He pulled out a cord, which he used to attach his camera to the laptop, and clicked a few more things.

"Well, that explains why, last year, they labeled me as Elena." I slumped into a chair beside him and pulled one foot beneath me. He glanced at me sideways but didn't comment on the fact that I was staying. If he'd asked why, I wouldn't have had an answer.

"Hey, Elena's pretty hot. I'd take it as a compliment," he said. I shifted on my seat, trying not to read too much into his comment. Did he think I wasn't hot? Why did that thought make me upset? I tried to tell myself that no one would like to hear they weren't considered attractive. It had nothing to do with Logan himself or how hot *he* was. To most girls at least. Not me.

The door to the computer lab opened, and Logan and I jumped in our seats.

"Mia?" Ms. Lackey said. "You're not supposed to be here."

"Ummm." I hesitated. My heart beat loud in my ears, and I could almost picture my school record going up in flames. First detention, now this.

"She's with me," Logan said.

I felt my cheeks grow warm.

"I mean, she's here on my invitation. She was curious about my photography." He nudged me in the side and waggled his eyebrows. "She was dying to see my work."

Personally, I thought he was laying it on pretty thick. There was no way Ms. Lackey would buy that. But she surprised me by saying, "Oh, I guess that's all right then." She smiled in a way that made it seem like she suspected we were hiding something else, and inside, I wanted to die.

Then she walked over to the desk and started rummaging

through the papers there. "I think I left my phone here. Aha!" She held up a bright pink phone in triumph. "Okay, have a good weekend, and don't forget to shut the computer down when you leave."

She was gone before I even had a chance to realize I'd been holding my breath. I let it out in a whoosh.

"I totally saved you back there. You owe me." Logan poked me in the side.

"Do not," I said.

"Do so." His smile was so deep, his dimples were showing, and I felt my resolve weaken.

"Fine, fine. Thank you for saving me. There, you happy?"

He held his hand in the air, like he was waiting for something more. "And?"

"And?" I repeated. "I guess I sort of owe you. Maybe. What do you want?"

"Nope, I'm not going to say now. I get to hold it over you and call in a favor whenever I want."

I scowled. "Way to take advantage of the situation."

"Agreed?" he said, holding out his hand.

"Agreed." I sighed, shaking it.

I had a feeling I was going to regret this.

five

Elena straightened her skirt and then pushed her jacket into my arms. Robyn stood by my side, her eyes scanning the soccer field like it was some sort of complicated equation. I felt the same way.

"I'm going to grab some popcorn. Do something useful and watch my jacket, okay?" Elena asked before taking a step down the bleachers toward the concession stand at the edge of the soccer field. "Oh, and, Mia, I have a feeling you'll want to keep an eye on the announcer before the game starts," she threw over her shoulder. She turned back around so fast, I couldn't see her face, but her voice sounded strange to me. Maybe because no one could run down the bleachers without sounding like they had hiccups.

I'd dragged Robyn along for emotional support, since neither of us was exactly sporty. Even though I'd carpooled with Elena, I knew she'd spend most of her time at the game talking with people more popular than me. Hence the need for backup. Robyn had met us here, but she wasn't happy about it. She kept checking the time on her phone, like that might somehow speed up the game, which hadn't even started.

The bleachers were filling up now, and the soccer players were probably in the locker room doing whatever it was they did there, but that didn't stop me from craning my neck to look for Vince.

I'd emailed him yesterday, and nothing had come from it. The announcer wasn't doing anything interesting, despite Elena's strange advice, so I focused on finding a seat.

"Over there?" I pointed to a spot apart from the gathering crowd. The failure of my little email experiment yesterday made me want to pull my hair in front of my face and hide from all the students now glancing my way. I didn't need them mocking me any more for my outburst on the announcements. Even Elena had been acting strange around me.

I wondered if my email to Vince had gone to spam. A whole day had gone by, twenty-four hours in which he could have asked me out, but no. Nothing. All I could do was find a seat and pretend like it didn't matter all that much that I'd basically been publicly rejected. Because I'd announced my crush to the school, and Vince hadn't said a word.

Robyn gave me a sideways glance. "Sure, we can sit way back in the nosebleed section. It's not like I actually wanted to see the game or anything." She knew I was hiding out. Sometimes I hated how well she could read me.

"Be honest: You couldn't care less about watching the game," I said as we walked over to the bench in question. "You've checked your phone obsessively since getting here."

Good thing nothing had come of the email. I had big-time nightmares imagining Robyn's reaction, which made me regret all of yesterday's decisions 100 percent. Okay, more like 80 percent. She'd never let me live it down. Maybe there was still time for me to email Vince, explain I'd sent the wrong name, and then delete both emails so Robyn would never know. Part of me wondered if she'd already figured out what I'd done. Sure, I'd archived the email so it was no longer in her inbox, the place she kept her unanswered matchmaking applications. But how often did she check her old emails? And how could I not have considered that before?

I slumped to the bench and set Elena's jacket at our feet. My notebook lay unopened on my lap with a ballpoint pen attached. I didn't really need them. Staying up so late last night waiting for Vince to call had given me an opportunity to write not one, but two sports articles—one if they won, and one if they lost. They were basically just a profile of Vince and how amazing he was, so I didn't need many specifics of tonight's game. All I needed to do was insert the final score and a few random details and I'd be good to go. I'd even emailed them to myself so that I could submit them from the school in case Vince wanted to hang out after the game. A girl could dream, couldn't she?

Scanning the crowd, I tried not to notice how many people were looking in my direction.

"Ignore them," Robyn said, noticing my preoccupation. "Who cares what they think?"

"Easy for you to say," I muttered. Seriously, how was Robyn always so sure of herself? If someone told me purple hair was in style, I'd have dyed my own in a heartbeat.

A freshman I didn't know was staring me down, laughing with her friends. I quickly looked back at the field, feigning a sudden interest in the soccer net. Very convincing, I was sure. I was focusing so hard, I jumped when someone sat down beside me.

"What's so fascinating about the soccer goal?" Logan asked.

"Ummm . . ." I scooted an inch to my left, away from Logan, but Robyn's presence prevented me from going farther.

She didn't move over.

"The metal is so shiny, don't you think?" Mentally, I slapped myself. Seriously? *Shiny* was the best I could come up with?

Good one, my inner thoughts taunted.

Shut up, I thought back.

Logan raised his eyebrows but otherwise didn't do anything except to nod at Robyn. A camera hung from his neck—the big professional kind. He pulled it up to his eye and took a few shots of the field. Maybe he was testing the lighting. I heard photographers did things like that. The shutter sounded loud in the silence between us. Then he angled his body and took a few shots of my face before I could bat the camera away.

"Hey!" I said. "No fair. I didn't even do my hair today." Not true. Knowing I'd be seeing Vince, I had taken about an hour to make sure I looked perfect. "Besides, that's my bad side."

Logan chuckled. "You don't have a bad side."

Robyn elbowed me and was smiling so wide, she was giving off distinct Cheshire cat vibes.

My eyes dropped to my notebook as I tried to control the blush creeping up my neck. I shouldn't have felt flattered by his comment. Especially because he probably didn't even mean it. Logan began taking pictures of the students milling around, and I was spared from answering. People began filling the stands, and I fiddled with my notebook to avoid their stares. Robyn scrolled through Instagram, obviously pretending to check out of our conversation so Logan and I could talk more. Joke was on her, because I didn't think Logan and I had anything to talk about.

"So why'd you volunteer to take over Spencer's section? Do you even like sports?" Logan adjusted some of the settings on his camera.

"Sure," I said, eyeing our soccer team, which was running onto the field. Of course I liked what I saw there. I mean, I would probably like it a lot more if it were warmer outside. Or if I had a firmer grasp of what the rules were.

Okay, so maybe I didn't really like soccer, but so what?

"The game is about to start, so shush," I said.

"That's pretty much the exact opposite of what you're supposed to do at a sports game," Logan said, standing up and letting out a whoop. He pumped his fist in the air, and I grinned at how uninhibited he was. He was a lot like Robyn, in that neither of them seemed to care what anyone around them thought. But just because I liked that quality in my best friend didn't mean Logan and I would be good together. Not even close. Besides, Vince had the same kind of confidence. Plus an amazing body, which was like ten extra points in his favor.

The air pulsed with energy as the students around us cheered. I'd never been to a game before, but it was almost impossible not to feel optimistic here. Once Vince fell for me, everything would fall into place. That is, if the email hadn't gone to spam. My smile dropped again.

"Where's Vince?" I asked.

"What? Don't you recognize your soul mate?" Logan's voice dripped with sarcasm as he sat back down. Robyn shielded her eyes with a hand, searching through the players.

"Hey, they're all wearing the same uniform, so excuse me if they look alike," I said.

"You're the one who wanted to sit in the nosebleed section," Robyn said. "You can barely see anything from up here."

"Vince is number twelve, the one over there by the announcer." Logan pointed to the opposite side of the field, away from the majority of the players on the bench.

"What's he doing over there?" I asked. "Isn't the game supposed to start soon?"

"We still have a few minutes until the coin toss," Logan said, but his eyebrows were drawn together in confusion. I wasn't the only one wondering what Vince was up to.

Then Vince pulled a portable mic seemingly out of nowhere, and his voice echoed throughout the stadium.

"This one goes out to a very special lady," he said, and I felt like all the breath had been squeezed out of my lungs. Nervousness that he meant me. Nervousness that he *didn't*.

"Mia." He held a hand over his eyes to scan the bleachers, then he pointed directly at me. I remembered what Elena had said about watching the announcer, but my neighbor was still nowhere in sight for me to ask how she knew. The concession line snaked around the corner of the field, though, so chances were she'd been caught unawares by the force of teenage appetites. Either that or she'd found someone better to sit with, which was also a possibility.

Then Vince began to speak into the microphone again.

"Mia Taylor, she's the one. One who makes my heartbeat drum."

Oh. My. Word. It was *poetry*. Poetry put to a cheer. Vince even did a few kicks and halfhearted dance moves for good measure. A smile stretched across my face. It was kind of a tradition at our school to ask people to dances in big, over-the-top ways. Classes were often interrupted, and the more attention it got you on social media, the better. This meant Vince *had* gotten the email, and all my problems were about to be solved.

Maybe now people wouldn't stare at me with pity. Logan's face was a picture of disgust and incredulity, so I tried to ignore him. He was too rigid for a soccer game, sitting there like a statue. Robyn was eyeing me skeptically, and I wondered again how frequently she checked her archived emails. Did she know what I'd done? No. Because Robyn never hid her feelings, and if she knew, she'd definitely have feelings to express.

What had I done? Had I gotten Vince only to alienate my best friend? Why had I thought that was a good idea? There was no hiding it now. A panicked feeling bloomed from my chest, spreading from my core like a stain, and I stopped smiling.

"She's so hot, just need to say, that she takes my breath away. Homecoming's two weeks away, please be my date, what do you say?"

Everyone in the bleachers watched me as Vince did jazz hands. I could have done jazz hands right alongside him. Vince had asked me to homecoming! Sure, he was only doing it because he thought Robyn had matched us together, when in fact Robyn had no idea. And it made sense why he'd gone all out. He didn't have a reason to doubt her methods, not when two of his friends had been happily matched by her and were now disgustingly in love. Robyn wasn't convinced, though. She was watching me with furrowed brows.

I put a hand up to my cheek, and it felt like my entire face could roast a marshmallow. Vince was still standing there waiting for my answer, so when his eyes connected with mine, I hastily nodded my acceptance. He whooped into the microphone, and the audience burst into applause.

Turning to the crowd, he gave a lopsided smile that somehow made him look adorable and provocative at the same time. He waved to everyone like they were his personal fans come to watch him perform.

It took me a moment to realize that beside me, Logan and Robyn were the only ones not clapping.

"Well, that was . . . interesting," Logan said.

The rest of the crowd turned their attention away from me, and I felt myself breathe a bit easier.

Robyn made a sound in the back of her throat. "I hate to be the bearer of bad news, but maybe he asked you simply because he's trying to help you save face. You know, from the announcement thing?"

She turned to look at me, and I almost stopped breathing. She still hadn't figured it out.

"You mean like a pity date?" Logan asked. He shrugged, and I could feel his arm move next to mine. "No, Mia doesn't need those." I was already having a hard time getting my heartbeat under control, and Logan wasn't helping.

"Well, it's definitely the most romantic thing anyone has ever done for me," I said, letting out a shaky laugh.

"Romantic?" Logan asked. "You looked like you were going to pass out the entire time."

I played with the hem of my sleeve to avoid looking at him. I couldn't exactly mention why I'd looked so worried— because I thought Robyn would figure out what I'd done.

"Yes, well, isn't that kind of what romance is like?" I asked. "I mean, it's a rush, and it's scary, but somehow it's all worth it?" Or so I'd been told.

Both Robyn and Logan laughed.

"It's not supposed to be scary. It's supposed to be . . . whatever the opposite of scary is," Robyn said. "Romance is supposed to be like finding someone who knows things about you without you ever having to tell them. It should be like the one safe thing in this scary world. That's when you know it's right."

"Right," Logan said.

I looked between them. "You act like it's so easy." I expected this type of conversation from Robyn. She often waxed poetic about "the spark" and perfect couples. But Logan? The guy who couldn't even be bothered to brush his hair? What gave him the confidence to talk about love like he knew what to expect? I turned to face him.

"As if you even have a romantic bone in your body," I said.

"I can be romantic." He didn't pull back or look away.

His expression let me know he was totally invested in our conversation. It wasn't the distracted look of a guy who found something on his phone more interesting or of someone who was thinking of something else entirely, like I'd seen too many times with my friends' boyfriends. I wasn't used to this kind of attention from a guy, and I kind of hated myself for enjoying it. I was all too aware of the way he was looking at me and what it was doing to my insides. And how I *wasn't* supposed to feel that way about Logan.

"Mm-hmm," I said. "I'd like to see that."

What had possessed me to say that?

Robyn half choked on her gum.

"All right, you've forced my hand," Logan said. "Remember that favor you owe me? I'm calling it in now."

I tilted my head and thumped Robyn on the back a few times until she swatted my arm away. "You want me to . . . what? Say you've won the argument?" I asked.

Logan shook his head. "Nope. I want you to come with me."

"What? Now? The game just started."

He tapped my notebook.

"And judging from the way you haven't even opened your binder, you already have your article written. Am I right?"

I opened my mouth, but nothing came out.

"Robyn, you can text Mia the final score, right?" he asked.

"Hmmm-mmm," Robyn said, her attention once more focused on her phone. She was looking through her email. My pulse skyrocketed. Robyn was *checking her email*. The same email I'd tampered with. That email. And looking at the sheer volume of emails there, she wasn't scrolling through her inbox but her archived messages.

I had to get out of here.

"Great," Logan said. "My laptop is in my car, and you can submit your article that way. We can tether the data from my phone or something. I'll take a couple of photos now, and then a few more from the field when we've gotten down there."

He pulled out his camera to take a few more shots, and I was left scrambling for something to say. Should I go with him? It would put some distance between me and Robyn's email. That was a plus. But it would also put me in closer proximity to Logan, and that was definitely not a plus.

"But Vince just asked me out. I can't go do something . . . romantic . . . with you." Maybe I could find Elena, wherever she had disappeared to. I could hide out with her until Robyn's anger had blown over.

"He asked you to homecoming, Mia. That doesn't mean you're *dating*," Logan said. "I can't have you think some jock is the perfect example of romantic-ness."

"That's not a word," I said.

"You see, if you want to woo someone, you have to know the best way to go about it."

"'Woo someone'? What is this, the fifteen hundreds?" I asked. I almost looked to Robyn for affirmation but remembered she was checking her email, and I definitely didn't want to make eye contact with her right now.

"You have to know if someone likes public displays or if they'd rather do something more private."

I gulped. This conversation had gotten away from me.

"We're not going to be alone, are we?" Where was Elena? If I could find her in the crowd, I could make up an excuse to leave this conversation.

"It's a surprise," he said. "Do you trust me?"

He gazed into my eyes, and I couldn't remember what I was arguing about.

I looked to Robyn for backup, but she was still scrolling through her email, a scowl overtaking her face.

"Mia, this email—"

"Gotta go!" I said, pushing Logan out of the row.

He smiled and slung his camera over one arm.

"Great. Bye, Robyn."

I was out of options. Apparently I was going to be wooed whether I liked it or not.

six

Cotton candy was probably the best food ever invented. Don't get me wrong, chocolate came pretty close, but there was just something about eating pure sugar that made me happy.

I stuck my tongue out for Logan's inspection.

"Is it blue yet?" I asked.

"Yes," he laughed and playfully nudged me away.

"Hey," I said, "If you're going to try to *woo* me, you'll need to see every side of me, even the gross stuff." Talking out loud about his "flirting" didn't feel weird, because I was pretty sure he didn't mean anything by it. He was just proving a point. I blissfully shoved another piece of cotton candy into my mouth and let it melt. Already, Robyn had called me three times and texted more than I could count. She obviously knew, but I couldn't deal with it now. Every time I thought about her reaction, my heart squeezed and it became hard to breathe. It was better to put that argument off.

Logan ate his cotton candy with much more care, taking small pieces and placing them gently on his tongue.

"See, this just proves my point," he said. "You don't seem scared, and you're not nervous. I'd even go so far as to call you happy."

"How can anyone *not* be happy at the Pier?" I asked.

"Exactly."

"That's cheating," I said. "It's like going to Disneyland and asking someone to compare it to a dungeon." The Pier was the closest thing we had to big-town entertainment. It was technically in the next city over, a half-hour drive toward the coast, but since Athens didn't have any hot spots, we pretended it was ours.

"Ouch. Poor Vince. Don't worry, I won't tell him you compared his poetry cheer thing to being a prisoner."

"It's not that," I huffed. "It's just . . . Well, it's not fair that you want me to compare one poem to an entire night of lights, glitter, and cotton candy."

"Hey." He put himself directly in front of me. "If Vince had any sense, he could have seen that you're not the type for public displays and he could have taken you to the Pier instead. Don't blame me if he was only thinking of himself."

"How is writing me a poem thinking only of himself?" I honestly wanted to know. Logan was acting so serious about all this, his brows furrowed and his mouth set. It was kind of cute but mostly strange. He wasn't the type to be serious about anything, so why was this so important to him? Sure, Logan had teased me before, but I'd always thought that was simply part of his personality. Kind of like how he often waltzed into class late or cared more about his photography than he did his homework.

"Oh, come on, Mia," he said. "Vince thrives on attention. If you guys dated, you'd always have a spotlight on you. It wouldn't be relaxed. It wouldn't be easy. It wouldn't be like this."

Then he reached out and took hold of my hand.

He. Was. Holding. My. Hand. How could such a small thing seem big enough to fill every space of me? My fingertips burned with the contact, and Logan started stroking the back of my hand with his thumb. His hand enveloped mine completely, making mine seem small in comparison, but when I looked down, it was hard to see where his fingers ended and mine began.

I should have been upset.

I wasn't.

I tried to hide my smile by biting off another piece of cotton candy, but I was pretty sure Logan saw, because his mouth curved up, too. If I was being honest with myself, I actually liked . . . *this*. All of it. My brain couldn't wrap around it, because it didn't make any logical sense.

"So what's next on your agenda, Mr. Smooth?" I asked. I'd think more about all this later, when I had a chance to analyze it. Right now, all I knew was that it took my mind off the twenty or so text messages I'd gotten from Robyn in the last hour.

He laughed, like I'd hoped he would. The sound of it made my stomach flutter.

"The Ferris wheel," he said, and my stomach flopped for an entirely different reason.

Through the lights of the Ferris wheel, I could see various couples lit up in alternating flashes of red, then yellow, then blue. About 90 percent of them were glued together in the type of embrace that would normally never be allowed in public. There were different rules for public displays of affection when you were off the ground, I guessed.

The Ferris wheel rotated slowly, but still. *Kissing* was moving just a bit too fast for my taste. Plus, I had Vince to consider. Vince, who had finally asked me out. I'd waited so long for that to happen that it was like a dream come true.

At that moment, my phone dinged.

I pulled it from my pocket, releasing Logan's hand to do so. I shouldn't have gotten sucked in by his charm. Who was I kidding? Logan and I would never work.

"It's from Elena," I said, scanning the message. "I texted her for the score from the game. Man, she's really chewing me out for leaving early."

"I thought Robyn was going to send you the score?"

Yeah, I'd asked Elena. Because I wasn't sure Robyn would do me any favors after she found out what I'd done, and I wasn't about to open her messages.

"Oh, sometimes she forgets, so I wanted to be thorough," I said, hoping he wouldn't push the issue. "But I have the score now."

Logan started leading me to the main entrance of the Pier.

"No Ferris wheel?" I asked, the relief evident in my voice.

"Oh no, we'll come back for that," he said, and my nerves kicked in again. "We should submit your article now, since I know you'll kill me if you miss the deadline."

In spite of myself, I smiled a little. Logan really did know me well.

Back at his car, I took as long as possible updating my article, but there were only so many times someone could spell-check a six-hundred-word piece. Eventually I clicked SEND and tried to ignore the butterflies throwing a party in my stomach. Then I told Logan I was ready, which was such a lie.

Logan locked his car and once again took my hand like it was the most natural thing in the world. Was it supposed to feel this comfortable? I could pull away again, but, really, it wasn't like holding hands meant much.

The line for the Ferris wheel was short. All too soon, a guy was pulling down the bar and trapping me in the gondola with Logan.

I was hyperaware of how close Logan and I sat, the bar keeping me from putting more distance between us. A crazy, irrational part of me was tempted to see what kissing Logan might be like. Just to see. But I knew curiosity killed the cat, and I didn't need it killing my chances with Vince. Vince with his broad shoulders and charming smile.

The worker checked the latch and stepped back.

"You two have a good time," he said, a sly grin on his face.

At my side, Logan leaned slightly forward, and I twisted

in my seat to see his face, putting a little more distance between us.

"Why are you so anxious all of a sudden?" he asked.

"As if you don't know," I said. "As if you weren't planning this from the beginning."

Planning it from the beginning. I was suddenly hit with the thought that this had all been just another way to taunt me. I felt sick, and it wasn't from the motion of the Ferris wheel. I should have known.

"And just what do you think I'm planning?"

"Don't make me say it," I said, embarrassment making my hands flutter on the bar.

He raised his eyebrows but otherwise remained silent.

"Fine." I sighed. "It's common knowledge that the Ferris wheel is the place for . . . you know. *Kissing.*"

"And you're worried I'm going to try to kiss you?"

"Aren't you?" There was no use trying to contain my blush. My entire face could have substituted as a space heater.

"Relax, Mia," he said. "I'm not going to kiss you."

That statement didn't make me feel better. Because if Logan wasn't wanting to kiss me, maybe I truly *had* read him wrong. Maybe he really was taunting me, and I'd been the naïve little girl who'd fallen for it.

Vince wasn't the type to play games like that.

"What?" I asked, carefully controlling my voice.

"I said," he repeated slowly, "I'm not going to kiss you."

"I— But—" I couldn't believe it. Stupid Mia.

Logan tucked a piece of my hair behind my ear, leaving my skin warm where his fingers touched.

"Mia," he said. "A kiss at the top of the Ferris wheel? Way too cliché. Besides, it takes two to kiss, you know."

Half my brain was busy analyzing whether his statement meant he *wanted* to kiss me, and the other half was trying to picture Vince's face. Maybe then I wouldn't feel so flustered by every word coming out of Logan's mouth.

"You know," he said, "it's okay if you like me."

"Huh?" I asked. It was the best I could come up with, since I didn't seem to be forming coherent thoughts at the moment. He was leaning in close, and the only thing I could latch onto was that he smelled really, really good.

"I can tell you're fighting it," he said. "I'm just not sure why."

Looking deep in his eyes, I couldn't quite understand it myself.

"Ummm," I said. I turned away. "Wow, would you look at that view?"

We were at the top of the Ferris wheel, the Pier stretched out beneath us. The booths lit up the night sky, and everyone seemed a world away. Endless open air stretched out in front of us as we started our descent, and I felt like Logan and I were completely alone.

He took my hint and let the subject drop, but that didn't mean I stopped thinking about it. How could I *not* think about it?

"Okay," I said, turning to Logan. "You seem to know

everything about me, so it's only fair that I know more about you."

One corner of his mouth tugged up in a smile. "What do you want to know?"

"I don't know," I said. "Just tell me something. Something personal." Something that would prove me right. Something I could bring to Robyn as proof that we were totally incompatible.

He thought for a minute before answering.

"I have a sister who's a sophomore," he said. "She and I are pretty close. She set me up with one of her friends for homecoming last year because I didn't have the guts to ask out the girl I really liked."

I raised my eyebrows. "You know, I find that pretty hard to believe."

"Yes, well." He looked me directly in the eye. His concentrated gaze warmed my stomach and sent tingles through my skin. "This year I decided I should probably do something about it."

I looked down at my lap and tried to breathe evenly. It was hard to do.

Logan cleared his throat. "Let's see," he said. "What else should you know about me? I hate ducks, I'm not a morning person, and my favorite food is apple pie."

"You hate ducks?" I asked.

"They poop everywhere, they're obnoxiously loud, and they poop everywhere. Oh, and did I mention that they poop everywhere?"

"Yes." I laughed. "It might have come up."

"Oh, and I also think websites that automatically play ads are crazy annoying."

"Can't say I disagree with you there," I said. None of this made me dislike him, which was kind of the point of this whole exercise. The thought made me antsy. We were at the top of the Ferris wheel again, our gondola softly swaying in the open air.

"Tell me something else," I said. "Who's your favorite reporter?"

"I don't really follow the news," he answered. He said it simply, like he'd been commenting on the weather or saying Hollywood produced too many remakes.

I stared at him in shock. How could someone not follow the news?

This was it. The reason we could never be together. I couldn't be with such a monster.

But Logan only laughed. "What? I have other interests."

"Like photography."

Logan looked out over the Pier and gestured with his hand.

"I've never been good at school. Writing, reading, stuff like that. I'm more of a visual person. So capturing things in my lens—photography—comes easily to me. And I can capture moments like this," he said, waving toward the water. "That's actually what I was doing when I got detention. The lighting on the fall leaves was perfect, and I didn't want to miss it. Sometimes my photography makes me lose track of time." He shrugged. "Photography helps me remember special things. After my dad died, I wished I'd had more memories of us together." Logan's voice got softer when he said, "Every day, I feel like I remember him less." He shifted in his seat. "Photography is a way for me to freeze time, and when I look back, I can remember the good times." He paused. "Cheesy, huh?"

"Not cheesy," I said. I still couldn't believe he didn't pay attention to the news, but the way he described photography sounded pretty amazing, actually. "When did your dad die?"

"A year and a half ago. Cancer," Logan said, his voice soft.

"I'm so sorry." I didn't always get along with my parents, but I couldn't imagine a life without either one of them in it.

"It's . . . well, it's not okay. But I guess it taught me I need to experience life more, you know? Go for it. Life is too short."

"I guess I can understand that," I said. "It's part of why I want to be a journalist so bad."

"Yeah?"

I nodded, the night air caressing my cheeks. "Journalists get to see the world. You see, I have this plan. I'm going to be the first person in my family to go to college. Then I'm going to make the student paper and build up my résumé so I can get a job at the *New York Times*."

"That's amazing," Logan said. He was looking at me that way again—the way that made me think things I shouldn't.

And he kept doing it all night. At the photo booth, getting henna tattoos, turning in our tickets for a fluffy stuffed unicorn—it didn't matter what we were doing, Logan still managed to keep me guessing.

Later, when he drove me home, I felt surprisingly happy.

"Thanks," I said when he pulled into my driveway. "Tonight was great." I was surprised by how much I meant it. "You've proven your point about romatic-ness or whatever."

He smiled. "Night," he said. Then he leaned over and kissed me on the cheek, causing me to fumble with the door handle.

I made my way to the door and waved as he drove off. When I got inside, my mom was reading a book on the couch. It must have been a good one, because she didn't even glance up as I closed the door. If she had, I knew she would have asked me about the strange expression on my face.

"Good timing. Robyn just got here," my mom said, turning the page of her book. "She's waiting in your room."

I knew this night had been too good to be true.

seven

I didn't open my bedroom door right away. Instead I hovered outside and debated my options, like an actor rehearsing her lines in the wings.

There was still a one-percent chance she hadn't figured out what I'd done, right? Maybe I should lead with that. I pulled out my phone and scanned her texts. Nope, she definitely knew. And she was definitely furious.

As soon as I stepped inside my room, Robyn hit me with her worst: the cool, calm anger of someone who'd have no problem sneaking pink hair dye into your shampoo.

"Well, hello, 'best friend' who doesn't respond to my texts." She was lying on my bed, picking at her nails. She didn't look at me.

I shut the door behind me and guiltily came to sit by her side, but she didn't move her legs to make room. I sat awkwardly on the end, putting as much distance between us as I could.

"Care to explain yourself? Like why you've been blowing me off all night? How about you start there? No, wait, let's start with how Vince magically got an email *from me* saying that you were his perfect match." Robyn sat up and crossed her arms while she waited for me to reply.

I could claim amnesia. Or pretend like she'd been hacked.

But we both knew the truth—that I was dead meat.

"I'm sorry," I said, leaning against the wall and burying my face in my hands. "I panicked. Everyone was making fun of me after the announcements, and I didn't know how to deal."

Robyn was sitting right beside me, but I couldn't bear to look at her.

"Honestly, I thought it wouldn't be a big deal. So he asked me to homecoming, so what? Doesn't hurt anyone."

"Except me!" Robyn unfolded her arms. "My business! The girl who I was going to match him with. Vince himself. Logan. Do you need me to go on?"

"No," I muttered. "Look, I *am* sorry. I regretted it almost as soon as I sent the email. But there's nothing I can do about it now."

"Yes, there is." She fixed me with a solid stare. "You can email Vince back and fess up. *Now.*"

"Robyn, no." I stood up, pleading with my hands. "Talk about mortifying. Seriously, if you thought I was embarrassed before, just think about how I would feel if Vince found out. He'd ask someone else to homecoming and everyone would know he'd rejected me." If he dumped me now, after publicly asking me at the soccer game, I would be that pathetic girl in all the teen dance movies who gets a slushie dumped on her at the school dance because she was stupid enough to believe the popular guy would ever ask her out. I paused, scrambling for more reasons I couldn't tell Vince. "Plus it really wouldn't look good for your business," I added.

"Oh really? Why is that?" She arched an eyebrow and gave me an obviously skeptical smile.

I didn't know. I'd said it without thinking. But that seemed like my last lifeline, and I had to take it.

"Because . . ." I said, trying to buy time. Then the lightbulb turned on. "Because I'm sure Vince told a few people he only asked me because of your matchmaking business. He mentioned how impressed he was with his two friends, remember? So obviously they talk about that kind of thing. You *know* half the reason he's going all in with me is because he trusts you. How would it look if word got out you'd made a mistake?"

"*I* didn't," Robyn said, but I kept talking.

"But on the other hand, how amazing would it be for your business if I go to homecoming with Vince and he has a great time? He'd recommend you to everyone, and the applications would come pouring in. Plus, correct me if I'm wrong, but he's your first soccer player, right? You've been dying to tap into that market. If he says you're great, you'll get the whole team to line up, plus a lot of other athletes. You'd finally earn enough to buy a car."

She was seriously considering my words. I could see it in the way she was staring off into the distance.

"You think you could pull that off?" she said. "I mean, you're not really Vince's type. You might have to pretend to be someone you're not to make him stick around. It's not like Vince is a bad guy; he's just bad for you. And homecoming is two weeks away. I'm not sure you can last that long with him."

Of course I could. We'd be perfect for each other if we gave it a chance. Sure, I'd had fun with Logan tonight, but one night of fun didn't mean we were soul mates. Vince, on the other hand, was friends with my friends, which was a definite plus, and he looked like a Greek god. Maybe I didn't know him all that well, but I'd seen enough of his personality to know we had potential.

"Definitely. It's not like you claim to set people up for forever. So you just need to prove you were right in having him ask me to homecoming, and you'll have so many people shoving money in your locker that you won't be able to fit your books in there."

"Not a selling point, Mia."

I took a deep breath and sat back down on the bed, smoothing out my comforter like that could somehow settle the knots in my stomach.

"What I'm saying is, please don't make me email Vince. I'll make it work."

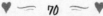

"You'd better," she said, frowning at her phone before putting it back in her pocket. Then she left, and I wondered how everything had gone so wrong so fast.

Vince called me the next evening.

"So," I said as I twisted a strand of hair around my finger. I didn't bother closing my bedroom door—my parents were at the symphony and wouldn't be back until late. "How'd you get my number?"

Way to go, Mia—that sounded accusatory. I winced. Talking to boys was approximately one thousand times more stressful than anything else in existence. And that included coming up with perfect headlines and being forced to work with cocky journalism photographers who refused to send you generic pictures. Any minute now, I would probably spontaneously combust from the sheer pressure of it all.

"I asked Elena for it after the game," he said. His husky voice made my heart beat erratically in my chest, and I sat down on my bed before I could do anything stupid, like trip on the math homework scattered all over my floor and fall out my window. Death by calculus. I couldn't imagine a worse way to go.

"Ah," I said. Yep, quite the conversationalist.

Vince talked about the game, and I chimed in whenever the moment warranted it. By the time he trailed off, I realized I didn't really have anything to add to the conversation.

Talking with Logan had been easy. So why was I struggling now?

"So," he said, breaking the awkward silence, "I was thinking that maybe I could pick you up tomorrow."

"Pick me up?"

"You know, for school? The place we're forced to go five days a week, seven hours a day?"

"Well, I usually try to get there a little early," I said, not wanting to admit just how big of a geek I really was. Sure, we were both overachievers in our different ways, but I had a feeling Vince wasn't the do-journalism-work-before-homeroom type.

"That's cool," he said. "That gives me more time to be with you."

Yeah, he was kind of missing the point. But still, he was sweet, right? I shouldn't feel annoyed. Or cornered.

"Okay," I conceded and gave him my address. It was silent on the other end except for the sound of a pencil scratching on paper.

"Got it," he said. "You live on the same block as Elena, huh?"

"Yeah," I said. "In fact, she's coming over soon to study French, so I should probably go—"

But he wasn't really listening to me.

"Have you ever been to one of her parties? I looked for you last night after the game."

"Ummm . . ." The truth was that Elena always invited me to her parties, but I never went. Her crowd involved a lot of people who didn't know I existed, and I didn't want to be the loser in the corner talking to the wall. Would Vince have noticed me if I'd actually gone to one of her parties? Or had he only asked me out now because "Robyn" had told him to?

The unasked question left a stone in my stomach.

"It's too bad she won't have another one until after homecoming," he said.

"Yeah, too bad."

The conversation stalled for a bit.

I was saved from having to comment further when the doorbell rang.

"Oh, Elena's here," I told Vince. I picked up my French book and started making my way to the front door.

"I'll see you tomorrow then?" he said.

"Yep," I said as I swung open the door. Elena stood outside, her inky dark hair illuminated by the porch light.

"Say hi to Elena for me," Vince said.

"Vince says hi," I repeated, surprised by the scowl that overtook Elena's features. Maybe they didn't get along as well as I'd thought.

"Hi back," she said, her voice clipped.

"Um . . . well, I gotta go, Vince. See you tomorrow morning."

"Can't wait." The flutters came back, and I smiled.

We hung up, and Elena stepped inside.

"You okay?" I asked as she sat down at the kitchen table. She took her time in opening her bag and removing her French book before answering.

"Yeah," she said. "Just remembering how crushed Vince looked after the game when he heard you'd left early. Where'd you go, anyway?"

"Huh," I said, plopping down next to her. "Vince didn't even mention it." I hoped to bypass the whole "Logan and the Pier" topic.

"Vince doesn't always talk about the things that are bothering him," she said. "If you two are going to be a thing, you should know that sometimes he can be kind of closed off."

I wasn't sure how to answer that. "Okay."

"He's my friend, and I want him to be happy, you know?" She paused. "Well, of course, you're my friend, too. I mean, I want you both to be happy, so don't blow it, okay?"

"Elena, he just asked me to homecoming. That doesn't mean we're dating."

"Yet."

Her comment gave me goose bumps. If he thought Robyn had matched us together . . . Some people really did jump into things quickly once they got her email, and I wondered if Vince would be that type of person. He said she'd done a great job with his friends, so the potential was there.

I placed my French book on the table, and together we turned to the chapter on subjunctive tense. Technically I didn't need to study it. I'd already memorized everything from that chapter. Our study sessions usually evolved into me tutoring Elena so she could spend most of her time focusing on drama.

"How'd your auditions go?" I asked.

"Fine. Callbacks are next week."

We studied for a while, and the whole time, she barely spoke a word that wasn't related to the homework. Usually she gossiped about the soccer team or what outfit she had her eye on. Hollywood and movies were typically hot topics, but now she didn't care about my latest Netflix binge or how many times her favorite celebrity had taken his shirt off in his newest movie.

After about half an hour of studying the subjunctive tense, someone rang the doorbell.

Logan was the last person I expected to see, especially standing next to another girl our age. A pretty girl.

"Here, you forgot this in my car last night," he said, holding out the stuffed unicorn. I took it with shaking hands.

"Um, thanks."

He opened his mouth like he was going to say more, so I spoke first.

"Sorry, now's not the best time. I'm studying with Elena." Plus, he was *with another girl*.

Angling the door so Elena couldn't see who I was talking to, I leaned on the doorframe. I shouldn't have bothered.

"Is that Logan?" she asked, coming around the corner. He gave a small wave in acknowledgment. "And his little sister. Well, what a surprise."

"Wait. She's your sister?"

"Guilty," she said, throwing a look at her brother. "Not by choice."

He nudged her with his elbow.

"Yeah, well, she's kind of annoying. Especially when she's nagging me about the girl I keep talking about. But Sadie's all I've got, so whatever. I guess she'll have to do."

Sadie spoke up. "You should have just told me it was Mia you've been talking about. I can't believe you kept that from me." She punched him on his shoulder, and he pretended to be hurt. "You didn't tell me her name because you knew I'd know her from the announcements, didn't you? Boys."

She directed this last comment at Elena and me. I gave a halfhearted smile in response. Thank goodness my parents weren't here to witness this awkward meeting. Then I'd have to explain why I looked like I was competing for an Olympic medal in blushing.

"You know, I had my suspicions after that whole pen thing," Sadie said. "I'm so glad he finally got the nerve to ask you out. It's been forever—"

"Oookay," Logan interrupted. "Well, it's been nice to chat, but we really ought to be going now." He started pushing Sadie back to his car. She brushed him off, ran to the passenger side, and hopped in before Logan had even taken three steps. He turned back and gave me a crooked smile. "Unless you need any help studying."

"French?" I asked, knowing full well Logan didn't take it.

"Oh," he said. "Yeah, no can do. I'll just let you . . ." He waved an arm in the air, motioning toward my kitchen and the books waiting for me there. "Well, bye. See you guys at school tomorrow."

I closed the door before he could say anything else incriminating.

Behind the closed door, Elena gave me *the look*. I ignored her and moved back to the kitchen table, hiding behind my French book. I put the unicorn beside me, hoping she wouldn't mention it.

For a long time, she didn't say anything at all.

"You left the game to go on a date with Logan," she said. It wasn't a question, so I didn't bother answering. If I thought she was being cold before, it was nothing like the frost coming off her now.

"So you and Logan are, what . . . together now?"

I shook my head and clasped my hands in my lap.

"That's not exactly fair to Vince, you know—whatever this thing with Logan is. I mean, it's not fair to Logan, either. You have two guys going after you, and you don't even have the decency to cut one of them loose. I never took you as the player type."

"I know," I moaned, putting my head on the table and crossing my arms on top. "It's a problem. But what should I do? I don't even know if Logan or Vince are serious about me. And it's not like I'm encouraging Logan. I've never had this happen before. Trust me, whatever I'm doing, it's innocent."

Her laugh was loud. "Oh, come on, Mia. I saw the way you looked at each other." She slammed her book shut, grabbed her water bottle, and walked over to the sink to refill it. "You know, of all my friends, you were always the one who cared about other people the most. I guess that's changed."

Where had that come from? My head jerked up, and I felt the sting hit straight to my gut. For a moment, I didn't have any words.

"It's not like I'm trying to hurt them," I finally said, keeping my eyes on the book in front of me. If I looked up, she'd probably see the tears pooling at the edges of my eyes, and I really didn't want her to think any less of me than she apparently already did. "Logan only asked me out yesterday—the same time Vince asked me to homecoming. I'm working on it, okay?" Couldn't she see I was in this situation *because* I was trying to be nice?

I shifted in my seat and flipped a page in my book. Elena came back to the table and sat across from me, rather than beside me, where she'd been sitting before. I wasn't sure if that was intentional, but the space felt larger than a swimming pool. She glared at the stuffed unicorn like it had personally insulted her. We both studied our textbooks for five minutes before either of us spoke.

"*Vous êtes une imbécile,*" she said.

"That's the formal 'you,'" I said. "We're friends, so it'd be '*tu es.*'" I paused. "Wait. Did you just call me an imbecile?"

She rolled her eyes.

"We're studying French, Mia, not how to passive-aggressively insult your friends."

Suddenly I wasn't so sure.

eight

Whoever invented Mondays should be shot. Only one week-end had passed since the soccer game, but it was like my life was on fast-forward. Was this feeling of whiplash normal? I'd been keeping up with my ordinary routine, but nothing seemed ordinary anymore.

I dragged myself out of bed and did my best to tame my hair. Not that it helped much. With a sigh, I pulled it back into a messy topknot and pretended that was what I'd been going for all along. I found a shirt I'd borrowed—stolen—from Robyn and paired it with my favorite jeans before making my way downstairs.

My dad prowled around the kitchen, opening one cabi-net after another, likely searching for something that wasn't low-cal or fat-free. Maybe he held out hope that my mom hadn't thrown everything away or that she'd overlooked some small shelf in her haste to get all the unhealthy food far, far away. I took a bran muffin from the basket on the counter and managed to take a bite without making a face. I had my hidden stash of the good stuff, but I wasn't about to let my dad find it.

"I still don't see why I have to suffer for your high cholesterol," I said, slumping into a chair.

He claimed a banana and sat next to me at the table.

"Mmph," he said in what could have passed for agreement.

He peeled his banana slowly and took a bite. "Your mother said something about homecoming?"

I swallowed while I thought about my answer.

"Yes, Vince asked me to homecoming," I said. It was easier than saying I'd betrayed my best friend and hijacked her email to trick Vince into asking me out.

"You said yes?"

"Yeah."

"He's a good kid?"

I rolled my eyes. "Yes, Dad."

"Good," he said, dropping the conversation.

I continued to chew my bran muffin. What would my dad say if he knew that was only the beginning? That Vince had asked me out because of a lie? Guilt took away my appetite, not that there was much of it to begin with. Appetite, that is. There was plenty of guilt to go around. Robyn said I had to make it work, so while I chewed, I came up with a game plan. I'd support Vince by going to every game. I'd figure out his likes and dislikes. I'd be A-plus girlfriend material.

Vince pulled into my driveway, and I said goodbye to my dad before he could ask any questions about the red sports car or the boy behind the wheel. I slid into the passenger seat and placed my bag at my feet.

The force of Vince's gaze drew my eyes up to him. He was gorgeous, as always. His smile could have melted butter, and I instantly became a pile of hormones and butterflies. It reminded me why I'd emailed him in the first place.

"Hey," I said.

"Hey yourself. You look great."

I raised a hand to my messy hair and tucked a stray piece behind my ear. "Thanks. You, uh, do, too." Smooth. That was me.

We didn't really talk for the rest of the drive, probably because I'd killed the mood with my awkwardness.

When we got out of the car, Vince put his hand on the small of my back. We reached the front doors and heads turned immediately. I saw a few people touch their cheeks while whispering with their friends, so I was sure my little pen act was still fresh in people's minds. Even the teachers stopped to look, and that was saying something. I racked my brain for an excuse to escape Vince's hand, because then maybe they wouldn't talk. Maybe they had figured out the reason behind Vince asking me out. Was I making things worse by acting like a couple? Would people stop staring at me if I weren't walking with the school's golden boy?

Then I realized I was being an idiot.

I'd gone to extremes to get Vince to like me, and now I

was thinking of reasons to dodge his advances? What was wrong with me? Why couldn't I just enjoy it?

I hated that I'd somehow let Logan into my head. Logan was a flirt. It wasn't like he meant anything by it. He didn't care about his education or future the way I did. I needed to get my priorities straight. Plus, I'd promised Robyn. I smiled up at Vince and leaned in a little bit. He took that as an invitation and brought his arm all the way around my waist.

We got to my locker, and Vince dropped his arm while I did the combination. I took my time opening it, my emotions twisting like the numbers on the lock.

"Oh man," he said while I put my books in my locker. "I forgot to ask Coach about our soccer schedule. I have a doctor's appointment tomorrow."

"Do you want to go talk to him now?" I sounded hopeful, which was ridiculous. But my gut was clenching with the memory of Robyn's words, and my hands felt suddenly sweaty. Why did Robyn think we wouldn't work?

Maybe it wouldn't be as easy as I'd thought to keep Vince interested for two weeks. And I needed him to stay interested, which meant I'd need to think of more conversation topics, for one thing. Just because he'd asked me out didn't mean I was in the clear—I still needed him to save my reputation and Robyn's business. He'd be the perfect boyfriend for me. I just needed to make sure he saw that.

"And stop talking to you? Never." He leaned against the lockers, crossing his arms on his chest in a way that made his pectorals flex. He grinned at me, fully aware of the way his stance put his body at its best advantage.

Maybe Vince already saw it. I didn't have to fake the smile that stretched across my face. Robyn was wrong—I could be myself and Vince would still like me for who I was, because we *were* a good match.

"Want to help me with my journalism article?" I asked, angling my body toward him. Vince was still smiling, but he cocked his head to the side.

"Is that what you were doing when you left the game on Saturday? Working on your article? Elena said she thought you already had it all written."

Should I lie? No, Elena already knew the truth, and apparently, she and Vince were best buds who braided each other's hair and kept no secrets.

"Uh, actually, I was with Logan."

Vince frowned, and I hurried to explain myself.

"I owed him. He caught me breaking into the computer lab after hours, and he was basically blackmailing me."

"Breaking into the computer lab? Man, you really are a nerd if you can't bear to leave school after hours," he said with a smile.

"I . . ." This conversation was going downhill. Vince smiled, but it wavered uncertainly, which made my stomach clench like a nutcracker.

"It's all good," he said. "You know what, though? On second thought, I really should talk to Coach before classes start. You work on your article, and I'll see you at lunch, yeah?"

"You sure?" I asked. "We could—"

"No worries," he cut in. "Really." His star smile was back

in place. He reached out, gave my hand a squeeze, and then disappeared down the hall.

I let out a gust of air and fell back against my locker. Elena was right—I needed to cut Logan loose. Vince hadn't started acting weird until I'd mentioned Logan's name, so it was all Logan's fault. This whole thing was making me crazy. I tried to remember what I'd been thinking before Logan took me on the date and why I thought Vince and I would be great together. Vince obviously cared about school and his extra-curriculars, which meant he was devoted. And that sort of thing was good for a relationship.

The morning passed slowly. Each class dragged on until I was sure someone was turning back the clocks. By the time lunch came around, I'd developed an eye twitch that rivaled my dad's when he'd had too much coffee.

I was at my locker, and I wasn't hiding. I was just . . . waiting for the crowds and the gossip to die down. Right.

"You okay?" Logan said by my ear, and I jumped.

"What? Oh, yeah, I'm fine," I lied. "Why?"

"Because your head has been stuck inside your locker for the last three minutes and you haven't come out for air. I was worried I'd need to send for a rescue crew."

"You've been watching me for three minutes? Why?"

He smiled. "Don't try to change the subject. Are you sure you're okay?"

I glanced around, all too aware of the other students milling in the hallway. Yes, I needed to talk with Logan, but I couldn't talk here.

"Yep," I sighed.

He narrowed his eyes at me. "If we went somewhere else, would you feel comfortable enough to tell me the truth?"

"Yes."

In a flash, he'd closed my locker door and was guiding me down the hall with a hand on my back. He stopped at an unmarked door and opened it, motioning me inside.

"A janitor's closet?" I said, looking around and seeing toiletries and cleaning supplies stacked against the wall. I stepped inside, and he shut the door behind us.

"Yeah. Now what's the matter?"

"I don't really want to talk about it," I said. Yes, we were alone now, but for some reason, that didn't make me want to break things off with him. Sort of the opposite, actually. I wanted to take his hand and pull him close. And even though *that* was a bad plan, my heartbeat picked up a notch and made my hands itch at my sides.

I studied the rows of cleaning supplies and bulk packages of toilet paper, as if that could somehow make me focus on something other than the fact that we were alone in a janitor's closet. I needed logic now more than ever, but around Logan, I didn't exactly want to be logical.

"You know, I think I know something that will take your mind off things." He was leaning close, and there wasn't that much room in the closet to begin with. This. This was why it was hard to think logically. I needed my mind *on* things. Not *off.*

Logan placed one hand on the wall behind me and took

a step forward. "I can also think of something that will help you feel better. They might even be the same thing."

How could he expect me to take him seriously when he said things like that? Obviously, Logan was simply trying to get a reaction out of me.

At least, I *thought* that was what he was doing.

He was even closer now, only a few inches away. He brought his face closer to mine, hovering just out of reach, as if waiting for what my response would be.

I forced myself to put my hands on his chest and push him away.

"That would just make my problems worse," I said with a small smile. I quickly pulled my hands back so I wasn't touching his chest.

His eyebrows drew together in confusion for a moment before smoothing out.

"You mean you still like Vince."

Now would be the perfect time to say something. To cut him loose. Especially if he was simply playing games.

So why wasn't I doing that?

"I . . . yes." Simply *wanting* to kiss Logan right now didn't mean it was a good idea. And surprisingly, I did want to kiss him.

I hated that I was so easily played. Especially when there was someone like Vince in the picture. Someone guaranteed to give me an honest shot, because he'd signed Robyn's contract. This thought calmed my stomach flutters, and I tried to give the same message to my mouth. I should be speaking up, not puckering up. *Get with the program, mouth.* But I couldn't get the words out.

I watched Logan's face for some indication of what he was thinking, but he was like one of those British guards who never twitched.

"You know what would really fix your problems?" he asked after a moment.

"What?"

"Figuring out what you really want." He smiled then, but I couldn't decipher it. I wasn't as good at reading him as he was at reading me, so I could only wonder whether he was imagining a kiss in his head the same way I was. "Or who. Because I'm not so sure you like Vince the way you say you do."

Logan ran a hand through his hair and hitched his backpack up on his shoulder.

"Just don't take too long, okay?" He opened the door. The words were on the tip of my tongue. I was going to tell him things could never happen between us. But he didn't give me a chance.

He left, and I was stuck pondering life's mysteries in a broom closet.

nine

Alone in the janitor's closet, I tried to sort things out. The way Logan acted didn't make sense to me. He'd been gone a whole thirty seconds, and still my heartbeat was dancing erratically. Was he trying to make me crazy? It certainly seemed like it. But why? What was his endgame?

I *knew* why Vince was interested. Logan, on the other hand . . . well, it was hard to trust a flirt. But judging by the way my thoughts kept drifting back to how he'd brushed his hair with his fingers, or how his voice sounded when he'd leaned in close, it was also incredibly hard to resist. Logically, I knew we weren't a good match. We were completely opposite, like when I tried to push the wrong sides of a magnet together. So how come I was having such a hard time pulling us apart?

Vince wasn't messing around. No matter how well Logan

seemed to know me, Vince was the one who'd asked me to homecoming. Vince was the one making a real move. Vince was the one for me.

So Logan wanted to play head games? Fine. He could play them with someone else.

Goodbye, bumbling, confused girl who changed her mind every other minute. I was the girl who knew what she wanted and set out to make it happen, and no teenage boy, no matter how tousled his hair was, was going to change that.

I squared my shoulders before placing my hand on the doorknob. That girl was going to make a comeback, and it was going to be epic.

I swung the door open and came face-to-face with Vince.

He stood with his arms crossed, and for the first time since I'd emailed him, he didn't look happy to see me.

This wasn't good.

"Uh," I said, slowly closing the door behind me. "Hi. What are you doing here?"

"We were going to meet for lunch, remember?" His shoulders were tense, making his shirt pull in all the right places. "I guess you forgot, though, because I saw you go into the janitor's closet with someone who looked a lot like Logan Sanders."

So. Not. Good.

"So what are we? Because I guess I thought we were official."

Guilt made my cheeks flush but then a spike of anger shoved all other emotions aside.

"Vince, we haven't held hands, and we haven't kissed. We haven't even talked about it. So how does that make us official?"

If I was going to turn down Logan, I needed to know where I stood with Vince. Sure, he seemed to trust Robyn and her matchmaking, but how far did that trust go?

An anxious feeling was creeping its way up my throat, strangling out all common sense. Any minute, Vince would realize his mistake and then he'd be out of here. I needed concrete answers, and I was nothing if not desperate, so I was going to push for them.

I wouldn't get another chance with Vince, so I had to make it work. This was my only shot—it wasn't like he would have noticed me without me pulling a few strings. I needed to forget about Logan and focus on Vince right now.

Vince, who still hadn't said anything.

"Okay," he finally said. "Fair enough." His shoulders relaxed slightly, and he reached out to touch my arm. "Sorry I overreacted."

My anger dissipated as we walked over to a bench in the hallway and sat down. He took my hand in his. People passed us on either side, and I couldn't help but wish there were somewhere a little less public we could talk. Vince was used to the spotlight, as Logan had said, so I guessed he didn't even notice.

"Have you . . ." He paused. "Have you done all those things with him?"

"What things?"

"Like, have you kissed him?"

"No!" I almost shouted the word. The last thing I needed right now was for Vince to get scared off. Robyn would kill me for ruining her business's reputation. Plus, I really wanted to see where things went with us.

"I guess this will be a shutout, then." Vince smiled and turned to me, taking my hand in his. "So what were your three conditions? Talk about it, hold hands, and kiss?"

"I—"

"Well, I call this talking about it, but I'll say it straight out if that's what you want. Mia, I think we should date for real. I want to give us a shot and go all in." He was practically quoting Robyn's contract. I would know—I'd helped her write it.

"I'm holding your hand now, so I guess that's checked off, which means there is only one more item on the agenda."

Before I could even think about what he'd said, he was leaning over and kissing me. There, in the middle of the hall. With our classmates all around. And our teachers.

A few guys hooted in response, some even going so far as to make suggestive comments that made my ears burn. I tried to ignore them and focus on the kiss. Because, hello! Vince was finally kissing me! And I was kissing him back. I'd dreamed of this moment ever since I'd first set eyes on his beautiful face. Sure, I'd always pictured it in a more romantic setting, but whatever. There were still sparks, and I knew more could come with time.

When Vince pulled back, he was giving me his brilliant smile.

He certainly seemed confident. And why shouldn't he be? He was, after all, gorgeous, talented, popular, and everything else a girl could want in a boyfriend. What *I* wanted.

"Listen, Mia, I think we'd be great together."

I expected him to mention Robyn. After all, she was the whole reason he'd asked me to the dance, but Vince didn't bring up my best friend. He let go of my hand and stood up. I felt the moment slipping away from me. "I'll talk to you later, okay? Tomorrow? When you've had a chance to think about everything I've said."

Why was he giving me space? Was that a good thing? Maybe it was bad. Maybe it meant he had doubts. Was I a bad kisser? Maybe my breath smelled.

I didn't know where I'd gone wrong. I was supposed to be making Vince fall madly in love with me, but nothing I did seemed to work out the way I expected. I was already failing, and soon Robyn would know. If Vince emailed her, would she tell him the truth? Would my public humiliation know no bounds? Would I be dateless for homecoming? I still thought Vince and I could work. We could be great together. How could I make him see that?

"The team does weights together on Tuesday mornings, so I won't be able to pick you up, but I'll catch you at lunch tomorrow? We can eat over by the locker rooms."

Smelly locker rooms? Okay, maybe Logan had a point when he said jocks weren't so good with romance.

"Great, see you then," I said, and Vince rewarded me with one of his smiles. He spotted someone down the hall and held up one of his fingers in the universal *wait a sec* gesture.

"Thanks, babe. See you tomorrow."

Babe? I tried not to make a face. He gave me a quick peck on the cheek and moved down the hall, where Elena was waiting for him. They were probably going to go eat lunch with their normal group because Vince was now giving me space. I smiled and waved at her, but she turned around without acknowledging me at all. I was used to Elena going all drama queen on others but never with me. Then again, a lot of things were changing lately, and maybe that was one more thing to add to the list.

Robyn was waiting for me in the lunchroom.

"I know something you don't know," she sang, tossing me an apple. We found seats, and I pulled out my sandwich. Robyn popped open her drink and took a long swallow. "It's about Mr. Quince."

She was the lucky one who got our journalism teacher for homeroom. I was stuck with Mr. Good, who was anything but.

I bit into my sandwich. "What?"

She frowned. "You could show a bit more enthusiasm. I've been waiting all morning to tell you this."

"Sorry," I said around a mouthful. It was hard to get

worked up about my journalism teacher when the ground was shifting under my feet.

"Whatever. Trust me, you'll love this. You know how our newspaper readership has been down?"

"I'm supposed to love that?" The possibility of our paper shutting down was the last thing I needed to hear about right now.

"Hush and listen. So Mr. Quince decided to run a contest. The person who can bring in the most readers for this whole month will get an internship spot at the *Athens Daily Chronicle* over the summer."

I stopped chewing. A journalism internship would be perfect for my college applications. I needed this more than I needed air.

"How will he know who's bringing in the most readers?" I asked, setting the sandwich down.

"He can track page views on the digital version. Fewer people read the physical copies, so I guess he'll let those ones slide." Robyn opened her bag of chips and crammed a few into her mouth.

That was true: Most students preferred the digital version. So Mr. Quince's method made sense, even if I did hate the idea of letting even a few readers go unrecorded.

"An internship at the Athens paper—that's pretty exciting, don't you think?" I asked. The wheels were already turning as I considered the possibilities. Step one, land this internship. Step two, snag a spot on a college paper. Mr. Quince always said that getting experience and knowing the right people were crazy important to a journalism career, so this was a no-brainer.

Robyn shrugged. "For someone like you, maybe. I have better things to do this summer. Hopefully." She ate more potato chips, chewing on them noisily, but I was too focused to be bothered by her table manners. Weird, though—what summer plans hadn't she told me about?

"So I have a month?" I asked.

"Technically less than that. It's retroactive for this whole month of October. He's already written the top three leaders on his board, and he'll announce the winner by homecoming."

As if I didn't have enough on my mind about homecoming. Why did that date have so many repercussions?

"Am I on the board?" I asked, leaning forward in my seat, food forgotten.

Robyn waggled her eyebrows. "Third place. Elena's first, and Joey's in second with his comic." She was smiling too much. Probably because of Joey. She wouldn't admit it, but I was pretty sure she was crushing on him.

"Whose side are you on, anyway?"

She dismissed my concern with a wave of her hand. "Yours, of course. I certainly don't want it for myself."

I squinted at her, but she calmly took a drink like she had nothing to hide. And maybe she didn't.

I sat back. How could I possibly beat Elena's gossip column? Especially with only a few weeks left? Gossip was what fueled our high school. *Everyone* read her column. I wrote for the opinion section, which was popular enough, but it wasn't even featured on the front page. And Joey's comic was brilliant. There were people reading it online who weren't even going to our school.

Someone sat down beside me and I jumped.

"Logan." I laughed nervously. I was so not prepared to face him yet. He'd just left me in a broom closet approximately twenty minutes ago. Twenty minutes was not enough time to sort through all the thoughts competing in my head.

He held his hands up like he was surrendering.

"Don't freak out. I'm not here to make you uncomfortable."

Too late.

"You hear about the journalism competition?" he asked.

I nodded.

"Okay, so I want to help. What's your next article about? I'll make sure you have a killer photo to match."

I couldn't help myself. I smiled. Even if he didn't love the paper, he cared that I did.

"Vending machine options," I said. "So really any random picture of the vending machines will do."

"Where's the creativity in that?" he asked, smirking.

"Oh, as if you have a better idea?" It wasn't like my article lent itself to many options.

In answer, Logan reached across me, his arm brushing against mine. He grabbed my apple and brought it in front of him. Then he stole Robyn's chips. Logan took a few more random items of food from his backpack, like a Twix bar and a can of soda. I wasn't about to let him see how curious I was, so I picked at my nails and acted like I saw this kind of thing every day.

Logan pulled a permanent marker out if his backpack, and he began to draw faces on the food. The apple looked horrified. The soda became predatory. The chips seemed smug. Then he arranged the items on the table in front of him, positioning them so all the food looked like it was attacking the apple, which was the only healthy thing there.

Okay, that was kind of brilliant. Not that I'd admit that to him. But yeah, it was a hundred times better than a picture of a boring old vending machine. Maybe I really did need his help with this competition. We'd have to spend more time together.

I shouldn't have felt so excited about that.

Logan snapped a few pictures, making adjustments on his camera as he went. He stood up, put his camera back in its case, and tossed the apple back to me with a grin.

"Catch you later."

Then he walked away like he hadn't done anything out of the ordinary.

I twirled the stem of the apple until it broke off.

Boys. Journalism. Internships. Everything swirled around in my brain, refusing to play nice. My fingers itched to pick up a pen and make a list—something that would make sense. But even that wouldn't really solve things. I released the apple only to find I'd left sharp nail marks in its other-wise unblemished side. I stared at the tiny moons, the edges of the apple silently bleeding. There was no way around this. No matter what I did, someone was going to get hurt.

ten

By Tuesday morning, I had a plan. Vince was my best bet, so it was about time I started acting like it. I was the one who'd orchestrated all this, so I had to see it through. This was my only chance with him.

The thing was—I wasn't prepared for the way that decision actually hurt. I blamed Logan's wavy hair and the way he made me laugh. His stupid grin. Most importantly, the way all the nerve endings in my body seemed alert to his presence, firing along my limbs until every part of me felt electrified and alive.

But right now, those things were gone and all I felt was empty, because I knew today I had to rip off the Band-Aid. But so what? I was about to get something so much better. Like a boy who actually cared about his grades and his future. Someone who wasn't playing me and who was perfect boyfriend material.

Last night I'd made a pros-and-cons list like Robyn had suggested. In between homework I wrote it out, comparing the two boys in my life. Everything on my list pointed to Vince—Logan might be flirty, and, okay, he had a nice smile. But Vince was actually being genuine. Vince was the one who didn't try to hide us away in broom closets and secluded Ferris wheels. Vince was open and honest, even asking me out publicly and kissing me in hallways. Even if that did make things awkward, it definitely made a statement. Vince was serious. About his future. About me.

Robyn was right about the pros-and-cons list, even if she was wrong about the results. Seeing it on paper helped settle my mind, and I knew what I had to do.

I passed the office and heard footsteps behind me. Before I could turn around, I felt someone whack the back of my head with a rolled-up newspaper.

"Seriously?" I said and turned to face a girl I'd never met before. Her lower lip quivered and tears started to pool in her eyes. She threw the newspaper at my feet and ran away, clutching her backpack strap like it was a life preserver.

I stared after her in amazement. Slowly I bent over and picked up the newspaper. I hadn't thought my opinion piece was that controversial, but obviously she felt strongly about vending machine options.

I shook my head and continued walking toward journalism. There were fifteen minutes until homeroom, and I wasn't about to spend more quality time with Mr. Good if I could help it.

A few people shot me dirty looks, and I quickened my pace. Had I submitted the wrong article by mistake? Maybe I'd accidentally sent in my piece on school uniforms or the one encouraging the school district to consider earlier school hours.

I opened the newspaper as I walked, turning the pages until I came to my column. It was the right article. So why was everyone giving me the cold shoulder? One boy booed at me when I passed, and I clenched my fist, crumpling the newspaper in the process. I rounded the corner and breathed a sigh of relief when I saw the journalism door up ahead. I stopped a few feet away when I heard raised voices coming from inside.

"The one time, the *only* time I don't review your column, you pull this?" Mr. Quince sounded furious. "You were late on the deadline, so I let it slide without review, but I can't believe you would print something this malicious."

"It's a gossip column, Mr. Quince. It's supposed to stir the pot." It was Elena's voice, and I unclenched my fingers from the newspaper so I could turn to her column. What mess had Elena gotten herself into now?

"Tame gossip, yes. Spiteful and vindictive hearsay, no." I could almost imagine Mr. Quince running a hand through his hair like he did whenever he was upset. "You're supposed to write articles on which students might be running for election or whether or not the cafeteria will get a soft-serve ice-cream machine. You're not supposed to write pieces that paint a student as a player. This isn't *Beverly Hills 90210*. Did you even have a reliable source?" His voice was getting dangerously loud, and I couldn't turn the pages of the newspaper fast enough.

"Vince told me himself. He needed a shoulder to cry on."

Mr. Quince scoffed. "And the word of an upset almost-boyfriend is completely accurate."

I didn't catch what Elena said next, because I had finally found her article and all the other sounds were muted to a low buzz.

> *You think you know someone. You might even think*
> *they're your friend.*
>> *But you're wrong.*
>> *Friends don't use you for your popularity or desert*
> *you when they find someone better. They don't lie to*
> *your face or sneak around behind your back.*
>> *Those aren't friends.*
>> *They aren't good girlfriends, either.*

I swallowed down acid and put a shaky hand to my forehead. I tried to think logically, but black was creeping in on all corners of my vision, and I couldn't help but feel lost. Betrayed.

I shouldn't have been surprised that being connected to Vince had made me a prime target for gossip. Still, it hurt that Elena had been the one to drag my name down. True, my actual name wasn't mentioned, but with the sprinkling of "facts" throughout the article, it wouldn't take a genius to

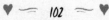

connect the dots. And judging from the looks I'd gotten on the way here, people were already guessing that I was the "Friend Gone Wild." I snorted at the unoriginal title. It was easier to mock it than to take it in. Anger was better. Angry people didn't cry.

Mr. Quince was being nice when he called the article spiteful. It called me a player and destroyed everyone in its path. It even slammed Robyn for setting Vince up with someone like me. It hinted heavily that a certain matchmaker had blessed the union with Vince, which wasn't fair. Then again, none of this was fair.

The back of my throat stung, and I had to resist the urge to tear up the paper then and there. I had to read the rest, even if it made me want to claw Elena's eyes out.

None of it was good, and it kept going for far longer than I would have liked. Unfortunately, I had to hand it to her: Elena was a very good writer. If I didn't know the truth, I'd be raising my pitchfork like everyone else. Her flair for the dramatic was evident in every line, stretching things well past the realm of reality. My eyes scanned the article again, looking for Logan's name in case I'd accidentally missed it earlier, but thankfully, Elena had left out anything that could identify him. That was a small consolation, though. Elena had dealt plenty of damage even without mentioning any names.

The newspaper shook in my hands, and I crumpled it up as small as it would go. That didn't give me enough satisfaction, so I threw it. Hard. It bounced against the wall and fell to the ground with an anticlimactic *thud*. I pressed my palms against my eyes, willing myself not to cry, but the blood rushing through my ears was more out of anger than embarrassment. This was so not okay. How could she?

I felt my face flush with heat just as Elena slammed the journalism door and brushed past me on her way down the hall. Her eyes glanced at me for only a moment, but I could have sworn I saw some remorse there. Not like it mattered. She could flunk French all on her own, because I certainly wasn't going to help her anymore.

I debated whether to go into the journalism room or not, but at least I knew Mr. Quince was on my side. Everyone in the hall was watching me, so I ducked inside and hoped Mr. Quince wouldn't bring it up. Yeah, right.

"Mia, I'm so sorry—" he began.

"I don't want to talk about it," I said, cutting him off.

"I didn't know. There will be repercussions for Elena. She's disqualified from the competition. I promise I'll—"

"No, really. I don't want to talk about it."

He gave a short nod and retreated to his desk, where he acted like he was busy, but I knew better. He kept sneaking glances in my direction, monitoring my progress as I strode across the room and pulled a laptop from the rack. I felt his eyes as I sat down at my table and then as I moved from the spot I usually shared with Elena. Even with her gone, I didn't want that table anymore. Robyn usually sat on my other side, so I skipped a chair and claimed Megan's seat. Hopefully when journalism class came around, Megan would be willing to make the change permanent. Ah, who was I kidding? I was totally skipping eighth period later today.

While waiting for the laptop to boot up, I looked over to where the newspapers were usually stacked near the door. The bin was empty, which meant Mr. Quince must have destroyed as many as he could—even though that couldn't be good for the paper. But enough people had read the article already that I'd never stand a chance of stopping the rumors. Plus, the internet was forever. Even if Mr. Quince had taken her article down, students probably took screenshots.

I was supposed to meet Robyn at our lockers this morning, but braving the halls was the last thing I wanted to do right now. I pulled out my phone to text her instead.

—Hanging out in the journalism room. Forgot to ask Mr. Quince something about my next article.

Hopefully she wouldn't ask what, because I had no idea. It was only a matter of time before she'd find out what had happened, but I didn't want to be the one to tell her. A nagging voice in my head said Robyn might take Elena's side. After all, I'd gone behind Robyn's back, so now this was evening the score. Maybe Robyn would be next in line and she'd turn on me, too. Just like everyone else in the school.

The screen blurred in front of me, and I struggled not to cry. How was I ever going to leave this room?

The phone at Mr. Quince's desk rang as I clicked open an email. I read the same sentence five times, blinking through the tears and trying to force my brain to function. The sound of Mr. Quince clearing his throat broke my concentration, though, and I looked up.

"That was Ms. Poly. She wants you to come to her office before homeroom."

I shrank lower in my seat.

"Why does the guidance counselor want to see me?" I asked.

"She only wants to make sure you're okay. She thought you might not be coping well. I mean, I might have let her know you're hiding out here . . ." He gave an apologetic shrug, and I closed the laptop a little harder than I intended.

Mr. Quince didn't say anything as I shoved the laptop back onto the rack and walked to the door. When I hesitated, he gave me a slight smile before bending his head back over his work. I opened the door and tried not to hold my breath, expecting the worst.

I was right.

Students glared as I walked to Ms. Poly's office. No one spoke to me. I grasped the strap of my bag and tried not to look anyone in the eye. By the time I made it to the guidance counselor's office, my shoulder muscles were tense and I had a headache the size of Vince's biceps.

The door to Ms. Poly's office was wide open as she sat at her desk and typed. I knocked and stepped through the doorway. She motioned me in.

I sat down and tried not to show my discomfort.

"You must be Mia . . ." She looked down at the newspaper in front of her, and I swallowed.

"Taylor," I supplied when she didn't immediately find it. I didn't need her reading any more of that newspaper than necessary.

"Right. I recognize you from the school announcements."

My cheeks flamed. I wasn't sure whether she was intentionally reminding me of the pen incident, but I couldn't help but feel the shame. Apparently, I was bound to be the center of school gossip no matter what I did—or didn't do, for that matter.

I only nodded in reply, because suddenly I didn't trust my voice.

"How do you feel?"

To my intense embarrassment, I started to cry. Everything I'd been so carefully controlling spilled out of me now, burning hot down my cheeks. I wrapped my arms around my middle, trying desperately to rein it in, but the tears only came harder. How come I could control every other aspect of my life, only to have things come tumbling down now, when I needed that control the most?

Ms. Poly reached across the desk, a box of Kleenex in her hand, and I accepted it with shaking fingers. I heard the bell ring, announcing the start of homeroom, and I hiccuped.

"I'll be late for class," I said, wiping at my mascara. Too bad raccoon-eyes weren't in fashion since I was pretty sure I'd gone well past smoky-eye territory.

Ms. Poly pushed her glasses on top of her head.

"Do you really want to go to class?"

My laugh turned into another hiccup, and I shook my head.

"Do you have any tests today or papers due?"

I nodded. "I have an essay due in AP English."

"Do you have it with you?"

I nodded and pulled it from my bag, a few tears dropping onto the top page and smearing the ink. She placed it on her desk and folded her arms on top of it.

"I'll get it to your teacher. You're excused for the remainder of the day, Mia. Go home and get some rest. Tomorrow will be better."

This only made me cry harder, since I knew it wasn't true. Ms. Poly came around the desk and rested a hand on my shoulder.

"Mr. Quince told me they'll be publishing a retraction in the next paper. Elena will let everyone know that her article wasn't based on fact and she didn't have a reliable witness. This will blow over. Just give it time."

"Th-thanks," I stuttered. It was a nice thought, but I was 100 percent sure she was saying it to be nice. She knew more than anyone how high schoolers could be. Unfortunately, I was getting a firsthand demonstration, and it looked like it'd only get worse before it got better. A lot worse.

eleven

My phone buzzed angrily, and I stared at the name on the screen. No way was I going to talk to Elena. I hadn't even answered Robyn's *We'll talk later* text and she hadn't been the one to do this to me. But as much as it ached, I could understand Robyn's anger. Elena's article was proof that my blunders with Vince were reflecting badly on her business. I hated that I'd been the one to let things get so out of control.

I couldn't bring myself to pick up Elena's call, though. I'd spent the whole day stewing over what she'd done, alternating between feeling depressed, furious, and embarrassed. She didn't leave a voicemail, and I couldn't decide if that was good or bad. All my emotions bounced around like a fruit cocktail of angst, swirling together until I could no longer determine which one was what.

A second later, I got a text.

—Sorry.

I didn't bother responding.

Then my phone buzzed with one text after another, like Elena had an entire novel saved up and she couldn't wait to see just how many texts "unlimited" really meant.

> *—I was mad at you, but I didn't think people would act like this.*
> *—I was trying to get lots of page views for the internship competition, but this wasn't the way to do it.*
> *—I guess I thought it was ok since I called it gossip.*
> *—But it wasn't.*

I snorted at the screen. So just because she called it gossip, she thought her words wouldn't hurt? Besides, why was she mad? I hadn't done anything to her.

> *—I was jealous.*
> *—You have two guys who are crazy for you, and you didn't even seem to care. Most girls would kill for that.*
> *—I didn't think you were being fair to either of them, and I thought they deserved better. Vince is my friend and I really care about him.*
> *—But that's no excuse. I'm sorry. Really.*

I stared at my phone for a few more heartbeats, but no other texts came. I dropped back against my pillows and glanced at the clock. Seven thirty. I'd managed to go almost a whole day without feeling guilty over what I'd been doing to Vince and Logan, but now Elena had brought it all front and center.

Instead I tried to work on my next article for the internship competition, but all I had were a few halfhearted documents saved to my desktop. All of them were absolute garbage, which wasn't helping my anxiety levels. Stress gnawed at me from every direction, twisting my stomach like a roller coaster. On top of everything else, I couldn't help but be annoyed that my ability to write coherent sentences seemed to have abandoned me along with all rational thought. Because there *was* a rational answer to all this, and it made no sense to me why I couldn't just accept that and move on.

Someone knocked on my bedroom door, and I quickly sat up and fluffed my hair. I even plastered a smile on my face, like that would make a difference.

"You doing okay, honey?" My dad peeked inside. I mentally cursed the guidance counselor for calling my parents earlier in the day to let them know I was coming home. I didn't care whether it was standard procedure—it still made my life even more complicated than it already was.

"Yep!" I said cheerfully.

My dad's frown deepened by a fraction. "You sure?"

"Dad, it's okay, really. Elena texted me to apologize, and they're running a retraction in the paper's next issue. It'll all be fine." I didn't mention that none of that made any difference. The damage had already been done, and in the immortal words of Taylor Swift, "Band-Aids don't fix bullet holes." I stifled a sigh. "I think I want to get out for a bit. Is that okay?" There was no way I could stick around home with my parents hovering-slash-suffocating me the way they were. And I had something I needed to do.

My dad's face immediately brightened.

"You feel like getting out? That's great, Mia. Friends are just what you need right now. Be home by eleven. It's still a school night."

He disappeared around the corner, and I counted to ten before losing the phony smile. Throwing on a sweater, I hurried downstairs to the garage before he could change his mind. Or before I could.

I drove around for a while, taking the long way, with extra stoplights and turns. With each light, I went over my mental list. By the time I pulled into Logan's driveway, I was relatively sure I could do this. *Relatively* being the key word. I'd never had to do something like this before, and my hands shook on the steering wheel. I had to take a few deep breaths before opening the car door.

Maybe Logan didn't even care. Maybe he'd laugh and say he'd only been teasing.

That thought should have made me feel better.

It didn't.

Either way, this sucked. Option one: He'd been teasing, and I'd fallen for it. Option two: He'd been serious, and I was about to make his night a whole lot worse. There weren't really any winners here. Well, except for Vince, who was obviously the better choice in the long run. Because he fit with my friends and wanted to give us an honest shot. It'd be good for Robyn, too—her business, at least. And because I'd promised her I'd make it work, I didn't have any other options.

Logan's sidewalk seemed especially long as I approached the entryway. I knocked. A dog barked inside, and a few seconds later I heard someone fiddling with the lock on the door.

It was Logan's younger sister, and her smile when she saw me was like a punch to the gut.

"Mia!" she said. "I heard you got a little friendly with my brother in a broom closet."

"Yeah, um." I shifted my weight to the other foot. "Hi, Sadie. How's it going?"

"Great, thanks."

I nodded like I really cared, but at that moment, I saw Logan come up behind Sadie, and my stomach started doing gymnastic tricks.

"Mia," he said, softly elbowing Sadie out of the way. She gave a wave and disappeared inside. "I tried calling you a couple of times. Are you okay?"

I shrugged, and Logan immediately stepped forward and wrapped his arms around me. His chin rested on my head, and I breathed in his scent. He felt so solid. Exactly what I needed right now.

No. Hugs were a bad idea. Hugs made me feel all gooey and content.

I pulled away before my treacherous thoughts could short-circuit my brain. I was vulnerable from Elena's article—that was all. Vince would have done the same thing if I'd gone to his house first.

"Want to go for a walk?" I asked.

He reached inside the door, pulled a jacket off a hook, and put his arms through the sleeves. Then he pulled the door closed behind him and laced his fingers in mine. I let him. It was a type of sad goodbye before I ended things with Logan forever.

We walked down the block in silence. Streetlights dotted the way, casting a spotlight glow on the sidewalk. We were in our own world, the noises of the freeway far distant. The air was cool, hinting at winter around the corner, but with Logan's hand in mine, things seemed warmer. A few trees had already lost their leaves, the branches looking barren in the night sky, like they were reaching for things they couldn't have. It reminded me of myself, and I tried instead to think of Vince and how happy he'd be at my decision. Robyn, too, if it helped her matchmaking business. Me, because I'd finally be able to get to know Vince better and see just how great a fit we could be.

Maybe I didn't know him so well yet, but everything added up on paper, and I couldn't wait to prove my theory right. Reason trumps emotion, every time. Any good journalist had to trust the facts. Plus he had that face, and that alone tipped the scales in his favor. I mean, Vince belonged on a magazine cover or something.

We came to a playground, and Logan led me to the swings. We sat down, the chains clinking in the still air. Logan was the one to break the silence.

"I think I know what you're going to say."

I looked over at him and tried to memorize the way the park lights glinted off his dark hair.

"I wish it was something else," I said. "Really. But I kind of made my choice about Vince a long time ago."

Vince had let me know exactly where we stood. He wanted this relationship, too. Logan would treat a relationship the same way he treated school, like it was an afterthought or something that didn't matter all that much. I needed someone who actually followed through on his commitments. Someone with a plan for the future, who took himself, and us, seriously.

"And it has nothing to do with Elena's article? You're not doing this because you think it'll smooth things over at school?"

I couldn't look at him, though I could feel his gaze on me.

"I . . . I think you're a great guy, Logan. I do." I risked a glance in his direction to see him shaking his head.

"Then why're you doing this?"

I gave him a small smile. He didn't say it'd all been a joke, which meant maybe he really had been flirting with me all along. That realization made me fluttery, and I had to clasp my hands together to keep them from shaking.

"Elena has a lot to answer for, you know. It's amazing she has any friends at all, let alone her popularity."

"This isn't Elena's fault," I said. It was true. No matter what Elena had done, she hadn't been the one to create this mess. That fault lay entirely with me. And even though I wasn't about to sing "Kumbaya" and hold her hand anytime soon, I couldn't really blame Elena for calling me out on my mistakes. That was what she always did with people she was close to, and it was part of why we were friends. My problem was that she'd done it so publicly.

Logan's face was carefully controlled, but his eyes were intense. They were boring into me, searching for something. They made me feel more off-balance than I'd been even before coming here.

I stood up and put my hands in my pockets. Without Logan to warm them up, they were chillier.

"Things will be better this way," I said. "I promise."

Logan looked at me for a long moment, one side of his mouth curled up ever so slightly. I leaned over and lightly kissed his cheek. I shouldn't have, but I couldn't resist. Then I turned around and started walking back alone.

I'd only made it halfway to the sidewalk when I heard Logan call my name.

"I won't change my mind."

I walked away. It took all my willpower not to look back.

twelve

I was wrung dry like a towel, and all my emotions were now a puddle at my feet. After doing something so draining, I was entitled to a little ice cream. I took an extra-large spoonful. Not because I was sad or anything.

"I hate to say I told you so." Robyn crossed her arms and sat back in her seat. A mostly uneaten bowl of strawberry swirl sat in front of her, the sprinkles sliding off as it melted. "If you had listened to me back then, none of this would have happened, and my matchmaking business would be doing better right now." She was one to talk. She wouldn't even mention Joey's name, but she made gaga eyes at him every day in journalism. I'd tried bringing him up, but she kept brushing it off. She threw herself into her journalism articles, working on them every chance she got. But I was onto her.

"I thought you said you had so many applications, you

couldn't come with me to Vince's next game," I said, taking another spoonful of my mint chocolate chip. After I'd left Logan at the park, Robyn had followed through on her threat to "talk later." So I said we had to talk in an ice-cream shop. If she was going to chew me out, I needed comfort food on hand. Plus, I figured Robyn could proofread my next article for the competition once she was done. Too bad she wasn't exactly being helpful. Like, at all. She wouldn't even let me see the article she was working on. It was strange enough that she was writing actual articles rather than just her Dear Robyn answers. But why hadn't any of them been printed in the school paper? Things weren't adding up. So that meant she probably hated me and was hiding *something*.

"Yeah, until half of them demanded a refund. Elena's article did some serious damage. People don't want to hire me if I might set them up with a player." Robyn stuck her spoon in and played with the swirl, then scooped it off like a vengeful guillotine. "I'll never afford a car at this rate." She pointed the spoon at me. "And it's all your fault. I'll forever be stuck at home, the forgotten child who's only remembered when my parents need a babysitter."

"Don't worry; I promise things will get better from here," I said. "Vince asked me to be his girlfriend, and Logan is now out of the picture."

Robyn raised her eyebrows. "You seem thrilled."

"Robyn, trust me, I'm doing this for you." She'd asked me to make it work, and I never broke my promises. Now that people were demanding refunds, I had to prove them wrong, to show them how Vince and I were a great match.

She pointed her spoon at me. "No, you're doing this for *you*. It's like you have some kind of popular-person fantasy. It's messing with your head, so now you're saying no to the perfectly nice boy who's already head over heels for you."

I scoffed.

"Okay, maybe it's not a popularity thing," she said, "but it's some twisted urge to control everything. I always said your perfectionism would come back to bite you. You like the idea of Vince even if you don't really know him that well. The fact is, if you really were doing the right thing, you'd feel better about it."

"Relationships aren't always easy, you know," I argued. "They take work. Just because it isn't all rainbows and sprinkles doesn't mean it's not worth fighting for. And it's not always going to make you happy." I took a swipe at her sprinkles.

"Sure, sometimes relationships take work. But this is freaking high school, Mia. It's okay to have some fun. And trust me, relationships shouldn't be this hard from the beginning. It's not like you need to torture yourself. You're so type-A that you don't even see how relationships don't work with a death grip." She shook her head. "Sometimes I really wish you'd just *live*."

"I do live," I said, taking another spoonful of ice cream. "I live *more* because I am prepared. By controlling things now, I have lots of different options down the line. This includes my love life."

Robyn shook her head. "I'm not even sure we're speaking the same language. If Elena were here, she'd back me up on this and you know it."

"Turning down Logan is for the greater good," I said, ignoring what she'd said about Elena altogether. True, Elena was all for spontaneity. And she made things fun. But she didn't get an opinion on my life after what she'd pulled. Not for a while, at least. "I even made that pros-and-cons list like you suggested, and Vince was the clear winner."

"Oh really?" Robyn asked, her disbelief evident in her tone. "How come I don't believe you?"

I scowled. "What? I did." I pulled out my phone. I'd made the list in my school notebook, but I'd snapped a picture so I could carry it with me everywhere. In case I needed a reminder. "See?" I handed the phone over, and Robyn took it with a sigh.

She pinched the screen so it zoomed in. "You didn't even try. This is only comparing Logan's negatives to Vince's positives. That's hardly fair." She handed the phone back. "Maybe you had fun bashing Logan, but you were trying to prove your own point. That's journalistic bias right there."

"Not true. Believe me, this is what's good for the long run."

Robyn was silent for a minute. "How would you feel if someone meddled in your love life?" she asked. "Even if they felt it was for the greater good? In the long run?"

I ignored her question.

"That's beside the point. All I'm saying is, it's better this way. Trust me."

"Better. Really. So you're saying you'd be totally fine if Logan took someone else to homecoming?"

"I . . ." Swirling my ice cream around, I contemplated my

answer. "Yes?" That sounded too hesitant. Why could I never get my words to match up with my head? "Yes, definitely." There, that sounded more confident.

"Careful, Mia." Robyn took a slow bite. "Methinks thou doth protest too much."

"Really," I said. "I'd be fine with that."

"Give me your phone."

"Why?" I cradled my phone to my chest. "What are you going to do?" Maybe she wanted to see my list again. Probably not.

"What do you think I'm going to do?"

"No," I said, clutching my phone in a death grip. "This is immature."

"Who's the one being immature?" She sighed. "Fine, scout's honor, I promise I won't text Logan. Can I just see your phone?"

I passed it over hesitantly, my grip lingering so Robyn had to tug it free.

Then she did something so much worse than texting Logan.

She called him.

"What are you doing?" I shrieked, trying to grab my phone. She pulled back, hitting the speaker icon so I could hear the dreaded ring.

"We can't hang up now," she said. "He'll still know you called. Might as well put your money where your mouth is." Two rings.

I sat back in defeat. Fine. If she wanted to call him, she'd have to do all the talking. There was no way I'd say a word. Three rings.

Then a thought hit me. Was Robyn going to ask Logan to homecoming?

Maybe he wouldn't answer. I'd just dumped him in the park, after all. I wouldn't answer if it were me.

"Hello?" Logan's voice floated across the speaker. I froze. Robyn watched me, a smirk across her face. No one said anything for a moment. "Mia?"

Robyn raised her eyebrows and held out the phone. I shook my head vehemently. What did she expect me to say? *Sorry for breaking your heart?* Not. Going. To. Happen.

"It's Robyn, actually," Robyn said smoothly, bringing the phone closer to her mouth. There was a pause on the other end of the line.

"Hi, Robyn." He sounded confused, as he should be. *I* was confused.

"So, I was sitting here chatting with our girl Mia," Robyn said, twirling the spoon in her ice cream.

Mentally I winced. *Our girl Mia?* I wasn't his girl, and this was like rubbing salt in the wound. What had possessed my best friend?

"Did you know we were all going as a group to homecoming? Mia, Elena, and me? We haven't talked about the details yet."

I frowned. That had been the plan. Before we even had dates. Before Elena single-handedly destroyed my reputation. Now I wasn't sure I could stand to be in the same room as her, let alone make awkward small talk. I needed more time apart.

"Uh, no?" Logan said. I wondered what he was doing right now, what he looked like. Was he sweeping the hair off his forehead and staring off in the distance with his soulful brown eyes? Or was he smiling, dimples and all? And why did I care? I didn't. I totally didn't care.

"So I think it'd be fun if we all go together. As a group." Robyn set her spoon down.

"Are you asking me to be your date?" Logan's voice was slow, like he was struggling to process this conversation just as much as I was.

Robyn's eyes shot to mine. I don't know what she saw there, but her eyes immediately widened. I realized I was holding on to the table like my fingernails were claws, so I forced myself to release my grip and pick up the spoon instead, shoving another spoonful in my mouth.

"No!" Robyn practically spat the word, fumbling with the phone in the process. "No, I wasn't asking that."

"So you're saying I should ask Elena?"

I didn't know it was possible to choke on ice cream until it happened to me. I blamed the chocolate chips. Dangerous things, chocolate chips.

Robyn raised an eyebrow while I struggled to get control of myself.

"Well." She cleared her throat. "I thought maybe you could just join our group, but now that I think about it . . . I guess?"

The other end of the line was silent for a bit while I simply stared at Robyn.

"Uh, why?" Logan asked.

Robyn seemed to regain her composure, taking a deep breath and sitting up straight. She looked down at the phone, then back up to smile conspiratorially at me.

"Trust me. You know why they call me Cupid, don't you?" Robyn paused for dramatic effect. "It's because I know how to make sure people end up with their best match."

My eyes stung, which was stupid. But just because I had turned Logan down didn't mean Robyn had to match him with Elena. Even hearing her name made me bristle all over. Especially hearing *Logan* say her name. It was a fresh kind of torture, one that had me tensing up like I was braced for an attack. And it was Robyn's fault.

I guess I shouldn't have felt betrayed. Logan wasn't mine to get upset over.

Not anymore.

Not ever.

He was silent on the other end of the line while he thought about something. Was he actually considering it? I took another bite and scraped the bottom of my bowl. Empty.

"Don't you think, Mia?" Robyn's eyes bored into mine as she spoke into the phone. "Don't you think it'd be good if Logan asked someone else?"

I was pretty sure my eyes were bugging out of my head, like those squeaky toys I'd loved as a child, but I forced myself to answer with a bright tone. "Yes." It was the only word I could get out.

"Think about it, okay?" Robyn asked. "I'm going to text you my number from Mia's phone. We should talk. About ways you can ask Elena."

I needed more ice cream.

Logan took a long time responding. "Okay."

"Great. I'll talk to you later then."

Robyn hung up, and I was pretty sure I could feel smoke coming out of my ears. If ever there was a time for yoga breathing, this was it. Five seconds in and ten seconds out. In and out again. I clasped my shaking hands under my legs and repeated a new mantra to myself: "I. Am. Fine. With. This." Robyn was smirking as she typed her text, which meant she wasn't buying it.

Mentally, I calculated how much money I had in my bank account and whether I could afford more ice cream. Robyn passed me my phone.

"Elena? Really?" I'd promised myself I wouldn't say anything, but it slipped out before I could help it.

Robyn crossed her arms, but I thought I detected a hint of uncertainty behind her expression when she said, "You stole her homecoming date. It's only fair that she steals yours."

I sucked in a breath, but for once, I had no words.

thirteen

It was only Wednesday morning, but already I needed a weekend. Or a professional massage. Or maybe I needed to move someplace far away. Like Tahiti. Maybe there people wouldn't give me nasty looks and call me names when they thought I couldn't hear.

I made my way across the courtyard, eager to get to homeroom. I'd texted Vince last night and told him I wouldn't need a ride but would talk to him later. I'd even added a heart emoji so he wouldn't feel like I was blowing him off. I was trying to be as late to school as possible without actually being late, of course. The teachers were the only ones on my side, and I couldn't afford to alienate them. Even if they were paid to be nice to me.

What Robyn said—that I'd stolen Elena's homecoming date—still rattled around my brain, refusing to make sense with everything else I knew. So I shoved it to the corner, vowing to deal with it later. It kept poking at me, though, like an itchy tag in an already itchy sweater. But Elena had told me herself that they were only friends, which meant maybe Robyn was seeing things that weren't there. And Vince *had* submitted an application, which he probably wouldn't have done if he already knew who he liked. Right?

I wanted to ask Elena outright, then remembered we weren't exactly speaking at the moment. I was hit all over again with the loss. She'd have found a way to make me feel better, laugh all this off. But I didn't need to dwell on her any more than I did Logan.

I quickened my pace to get to the door connecting the courtyard to the rest of the school. A group of girls behind me were clustered in a small circle, their voices carrying enough that I knew they were talking about me.

"That's her," one of them said. I looked behind me to see if I recognized any of them. I didn't.

"What? Think you can do better? Vince isn't enough for you?" she called out to me. I ducked my head and tried to walk as quickly as possible.

With the momentum I had going, I shouldn't have been surprised when the door loomed up in front of me, but I was. And I smacked into it. Hard. There was no time for a graceful landing—I simply hit the grass and felt all the air leave my body. It only took about two seconds, but now I was staring up at the gray overcast sky and wondering if this day could get any worse.

The girls laughed, and I was glad I didn't know them. But then again, if I didn't know them, they were probably in a different grade. That meant students who were probably younger than me were openly mocking me, so that was great.

A hand reached into my field of vision, offering to help me up. I took it and tried to repair what dignity I could muster. Turning to the person who'd offered to help when mocking me would have been just as easy, I gave my first genuine smile of the day. It quickly turned to a frown.

"Logan? What are you doing here?" I asked. This was not supposed to happen. I'd rejected him and he was still being nice? I mean, that was great, and much preferable to the alternative, but still unexpected. Then again, I did need his photography creativity for the paper. Pictures were worth a thousand words and all that. I needed all the help I could get if I wanted any chance at that internship. So I needed to play nice, too. Maybe he had the right idea. I studied Logan's face. He looked good. Too good. I wasn't supposed to be thinking he looked good.

My eyes moved to his shirt instead. Much safer. But then I noticed how snugly his shirt fit over his muscles, and I stifled a groan. He was making this hard. Stupid boy for being hot. It was all his fault. And since when did I like the artsy look? Because, I realized as I resisted the urge to run my fingers through his messy hair, I did like it. A little too much.

I blushed and cleared my throat.

"Sorry," he said, and his voice sent shivers up and down my

arms. For a second I worried that he could read my thoughts. "I wasn't aware the courtyard was off-limits." He smiled, and I relaxed. We could be friends. That was all this was.

My reasons for breaking things off with him were still valid, and I kind of hated that I had to remind myself of that. Seriously, was I that weak? Well, with chocolate, yeah, hands down. But it wasn't like I ate it for every meal. I had some restraint.

If I could turn down a delicious truffle, I could do the same with Logan. It was all about willpower, and I totally had that. Vince was like a chocolate protein bar—packed with nutrients and enough flavor to satisfy my chocolate craving. Who needed truffles, anyway? I knew which one was better for me.

"I mean, hey, how's it going? What brings you here?" I knew I sounded lame.

"I was looking for you, actually."

Maybe we couldn't be friends. Not if he pushed the boundaries. I'd have to email him for pictures, like everyone else. Just because I logically knew what was better for me didn't mean my heart agreed. But that was easily fixed. I simply needed to spend more time with Vince and then things would feel more focused. Mind over matter.

I took a step back, putting more distance between us.

"Ummm." I coughed nervously. "Well, you found me."

Logan ran a hand through his hair, managing to make it look mussed and adorable all at once.

"Listen." He looked at the students milling around the

courtyard and pulled me to a secluded corner. Oh boy. An electric current seemed to reach between us, but I tried to ignore it.

My heart thudded against my chest, and I was hyper-aware of my hands. What was I supposed to be doing with my hands? They itched to reach out and fix a strand of his hair, but I clenched them tightly at my sides. That didn't seem to be enough, so I shoved them deep in my pockets.

Once upon a time, Logan had been only a nuisance to me. I had my lists. My reasons. They were good reasons, too. When we were apart, it was so easy to think of them. But when we were together, and when he was looking at me this way . . . Where was Vince when I needed him?

"I wanted to talk to you," he said. "Last night . . . last night I said I wouldn't change my mind, remember?"

As if I could forget. I nodded.

"Well, I feel like a total jerk for saying this, but I think it's only right for you to know." He took a deep breath and looked down at his shoes. "I think I might have . . . changed my mind." He looked at me then, and I felt a pang.

So soon? He'd gotten over me that quickly? And how? Who?

"I was thinking about what Robyn said last night, when she called me from your phone, and when we talked later, I could see that she was right. I'm going to ask Elena to the dance."

Elena?

Ice burned in my veins but was quickly replaced by

fire. I struggled to make sense of what Logan had just said, but it was hard to think clearly when I felt engulfed by flames.

But who was I to get upset? Or even confused? I shouldn't have felt blindsided by this announcement. Logan had said himself that he thought Elena was hot, back when he'd caught me in the computer lab. It'd been yet another reason I'd thought he was nothing but a flirt. And with the phone call last night, I should have expected this. Planned for it. I was the queen of planning.

"That's great, Logan." I swallowed. "It's better this way. Now you can go with Elena, and I can date Vince, and everyone can be happy."

So why didn't I feel more relieved?

He looked up from his shoes and palmed the back of his neck.

"Yeah. Elena is loud and kind of crazy, but I think she'd keep things interesting. I mean, Robyn helped me see that it has potential."

Potential? So this wasn't just for homecoming? Or some weird trick to get under my skin? He really was *interested* in Elena?

I drew in a breath, then slowly released it. But that didn't stop me from feeling suddenly dizzy.

Elena didn't deserve him. Even if we were friends. Sort of. Not as much anymore. Even if I could see all her positive attributes and why someone like Logan might like her.

It didn't matter if Logan and Elena had more in common.

Maybe. I tried to think logically, but it still felt like I'd been run over with this news.

I shook my head. I'd already made my choice. Now I had to see it through, no matter how much it made me see red. It wasn't like I could pick who Logan liked. But the thing that made it worse was that it was Elena—I totally got why guys were interested in her and I couldn't even fault them for it. She was my friend. Elena was serious competition. Then again, I shouldn't be competing. I wasn't.

The only competition I should be involved in was the one for the journalism internship. That was what I needed to focus on.

This was why Logan and I would never work. He short-circuited my brain and strangled out all common sense to the point where I couldn't think clearly. That was definitely a check in the negative column. I liked logic. Doing things that made sense. Having a plan. All the things Vince stood for.

"That's great, Logan. I'm happy for you." My smile was forced, but at least it was there. His smile, on the other hand, was overly big. Like he knew something I didn't.

"So," he said, all his characteristic swagger back, "I need your help with something."

It was like his smile had some kind of brainwashing control over me. Why'd he have to be so freaking adorable? I couldn't say no to this guy, especially after all I'd put him through. But if I had to be honest with myself, it wasn't my guilt that got to me. It was that smile.

"Sure, anything," I said.

"I need you to help me ask Elena out." He said it simply, like it was the most reasonable request ever.

"Wait, you want me to help you get Elena to go out with you? I don't think you'll need my help. I mean, you're . . . you."

"Yes, but she's *Elena*." He might as well have said, *She's ten times the girl you'll ever be.* I swallowed the bile reaching up my throat, threatening to choke me. I tried to ignore my emotions, but it was like they were a broken faucet that wouldn't turn off no matter how I tried.

"And we've never really talked," he said. "All I really know is she's pretty, and she seems like a lot of fun. You're her friend, so you can tell me what she likes."

He smiled again, and those dang dimples made their appearance. I squared my shoulders and gave him my best fake grin.

"Of course I'll help you out," I said. "That's what friends do." Something caught in my throat, and I turned it into a cough. "Elena really likes big, dramatic displays. So we should come up with some way of making sure you stand out."

"Stand out? You don't think my good looks have that covered?" He grinned, and I slugged him in the arm. Too bad I totally agreed with him. Then again, I had another hot guy waiting for me, and once I reminded myself of that little fact, I relaxed.

"She has play rehearsal today after school. Maybe you could do something then to ask her out?" I suggested.

Logan shook his head. "I've got tennis lessons after school."

"You play tennis?" I asked. "I didn't know that." That certainly explained his lean muscles.

Okay, I was totally not supposed to be thinking about his muscles.

"There's a lot about me you don't know," he said with a smirk. Robyn wondered how I had such a hard time believing Logan meant anything by his flirting? Well, this was exhibit A. Even when he wanted to ask out another girl, Logan couldn't turn off the charm if he tried.

I'd made the right choice.

"Okay, well, the student council is announcing the themes for spirit week today during the assembly," I said. Spirit week was next week. Already I was dreading whether I'd have to be a cowgirl for a day or a disco queen. Or, with my luck, probably both at the same time. I still hadn't figured out how wearing costumes for a week was supposed to boost school spirit for homecoming, but hey, who was I to judge? "It's during eighth period, right? That might be a good time to go for it."

"You said she likes big displays?" he asked, and I nodded. He gave a slow smile. "Then I think I might have a great idea for getting her attention."

The two-minute warning bell sounded, finally giving me an excuse to break off the conversation. With relief, I waved and made my way to homeroom, trying to ignore the knot in my stomach. By the time I made it to class, I'd almost convinced myself that I was over Logan.

Almost.

fourteen

Not all politicians are bad.

At least, that was what I *used* to think before Elena, the secretary of the student council, decided to stab me in the back with her gavel by writing that "gossip" article. This internship competition was already proving to be more trouble than it was worth. Half the people in our class used clickbait headlines simply to up their numbers, and I was pretty sure Elena had convinced her friends to hit refresh on all the articles but mine.

As I watched the student council set up for their assembly announcement, I tried to remind myself that some of them were actually quite nice. Even if they had instituted a pretty severe library-fine policy and banned chocolate from the vending machines. That last one still hurt.

The gym was somewhat full, and I couldn't see Logan

anywhere. Robyn was mysteriously absent as well. Vince stood near the bottom of the bleachers with some of the other soccer players, and I slowly wove my way through the crowd to reach his side. His friends gave me dirty looks before slapping Vince on the back and heading a few feet off to group together. When Vince turned to me, his expression softened.

"Hey," he said, an unspoken question hanging between us.

"Hey," I said as I reached out and took his hand. His face immediately lit up in a smile.

"You've made your choice then?"

I nodded. I could have done worse. Vince was attractive, popular, and the star of the soccer team. He was everyone's dream boyfriend. He'd been *my* dream boyfriend until Robyn had gotten into my head with all her talk of Logan being my perfect match. It should be easy enough to fall for him again now that Logan was saving his flirting for someone else. Robyn thought I only liked the idea of him? Well, now I could remedy that. Finally. I couldn't wait to see what else was hidden beneath all his muscles and golden-boy persona.

With a whoop, Vince picked me up and twirled me around. I buried my red cheeks in his shoulder and pretended we were twirling all alone, that we weren't in the front of the gym with a hundred students analyzing our relationship. Maybe fewer people would have stared if it weren't for Elena's article, but then again, maybe not. I'd simply have to get used to sharing his spotlight.

He set me back down but kept his arms around my waist.

"Glad you finally saw the light. I mean, it was obvious that I was the better choice."

"Cocky, aren't we?" I asked, resting my hands on his biceps. I could get used to those. I still couldn't wrap my brain around the fact that Robyn had planned on setting up Elena and Vince for homecoming. Sure, they were friends, but I thought that was it. Did that mean Elena liked him? Or that Vince . . . ?

No. Vince had asked me to be his girlfriend, and that had to mean something. Okay, maybe it had been Robyn's—well *my*—email that got things started. But he was still trying to give it a go, and that was an undisputable fact; any journalist would agree.

"Nah, just honest. Come on, let's sit down before the student council starts."

He led me back to his friends, and I felt a flash of pride. His group wasn't off-limits to me now. As Vince's girlfriend, they *had* to accept me. Hopefully this meant people at school would treat me with a little less hostility, even though Elena had smeared my reputation. Soon enough, my fellow students would see that Vince didn't believe the rumors, so they shouldn't, either. Then Robyn's business would pick back up and she wouldn't blame me anymore. At least, I could dream.

Robyn came through the gym doors and looked around. I waved at her from my spot at Vince's side, gesturing for her to join us. She shook her head, motioned to her journalism notebook to let me know she had an article to work on, then slipped back outside. She was doing that a lot lately.

At the center of the gym floor, Elena was arguing with a sophomore standing behind a table of sound equipment. From previous pep rallies and announcements, I recognized him as the techie guy in charge of the sound system.

Elena crossed her arms and took a deep breath, but she didn't step away from the table with all the sound equipment. The sophomore clicked a few more buttons on his computer, and music started playing through the overhead speakers.

From where I sat, I couldn't hear Elena over the music, but I could read her lips when she told him he had the wrong song. He shook his head and leaned back against the table.

People were watching the center of the gym now, but the student council members only stood around in confusion.

Someone at the bottom of the bleachers started *dancing*, and my attention snapped there like a magnet. It was Ron, the guy Tania had been quasi-dating for the last year. She talked about him nonstop whenever we prepped for the video announcements.

Then he was dancing *and* singing. He must have had a clipped-on mic, because I could hear his clear, strong voice, even with the music blaring. Someone else joined him, and then a few more people with each stanza. By the time they reached the chorus, a quarter of the audience was involved, streaming down to the gym floor.

A flash mob. This must be what Logan had been planning to get Elena's attention. I tried to evaluate how I felt about that, but then I reminded myself that I wasn't supposed to be encouraging my emotions, so I tried not to think or feel at all.

"What's the show choir doing?" Vince asked me. "This isn't exactly the best time to practice their routine."

"Ohhh," I said. "That's how they all know the same dance." That made a lot more sense than Logan teaching twenty people a complete dance in a single morning. Then again, if this was Logan's doing, where was he? I turned on the bench, craning my neck to look for him, but I shouldn't have bothered.

The crowd parted, and Logan stood in the middle. No, not stood—*danced*. Okay, maybe I was a little slow to recognize the people in the flash mob, but I knew for an absolute fact that Logan was not a part of the show choir.

Logan didn't sing with them, but he knew every step of the dance. Maybe he was a really big fan?

The members of the show choir began limiting their moves, doing more of a backup sway to Logan's center stage. The final chorus played, and Logan danced closer and closer to the center of the gym, where Elena stood with her arms across her chest.

Beside me, Vince tensed, probably angry on the student council's behalf. I knew he was pretty tight with Elena, after all. Or maybe he thought Logan was doing this for me, but it seemed pretty obvious that Logan's eyes were on Elena. Vince's hand almost crushed mine, and I had to untangle my fingers before they needed amputation. Robyn's words about stealing Elena's homecoming date swirled around my brain, haunting me.

As the last strains of music came over the speakers, Logan did a move that brought him to his knees, where he then put his hand under the table of sound equipment and brought out a paper sign. He knelt before Elena with the sign facing her, so I couldn't read what it said.

Elena's eyebrows crinkled together and she pursed her lips. Her eyes darted from the sign to find me. The anger in her gaze pinned me to the bench. Eventually she looked back to Logan, but not before the heat burned a hole where I sat. She gave a terse nod to Logan when the music was over, and everyone in the gym started clapping.

Elena grabbed a mic from the table of sound equipment and stepped to the front, effectively cutting Logan off. He didn't seem to mind. He gave me two thumbs-up before walking to the bleachers and sitting down. Watching our exchange, Elena glowered at me even more, if that were possible. Sheesh. What had I ever done to her? If anyone deserved to be angry, it was me. Here I'd been contemplating ways to make up with her, but she obviously was still firmly in the We Hate Mia camp.

I stared back, undeterred, and she grasped the mic like she was imagining it was my neck between her fingers. Vince looked between Elena and me, his questioning gaze making me feel self-conscious.

"Okay, let's get this party started!" Elena said, switching into drama mode. Her smile showed too many teeth, but that was probably part of her theater training. Music pumped through the speakers again, but this time, the familiar school song started playing.

"What was all that about?" Vince whispered in my ear.

"No idea," I answered. It was the truth. Elena had been jealous of the attention I was getting from Logan and Vince, so I had thought she'd jump at something like this. It didn't make sense that she'd be angry—especially at me.

After the song, the student council members announced the themes for spirit week, and I groaned. Pajama day I could do, but whoever thought togas were a good idea? Just because our town was named Athens didn't mean I wanted to be Greek for a day. Maybe I could get by with wearing gold bangles and some sandals. I didn't own anything with an animal print on it except for a bra I'd bought on a dare, so jungle day was a no-go, and there was no way I was going to do '80s day. Friday was the only other day I could really participate in, since our school colors weren't so bad.

Besides, I had bigger things to worry about than dressing up next week. My future career as a journalist depended on me writing killer articles that would bring in hundreds of page views, which wasn't coming easy. Especially if I'd need Logan's help with the pictures. Elena's little stunt had given her quite the lead, up until Mr. Quince disqualified her. I was still second place behind the comics, though, and I couldn't think of a way to beat them. Plus everyone hated me at school, and as much as it hurt to think about, I couldn't help but wonder *what if*. What if Robyn was right about Logan being the right guy for me? The question circled around and around in my head like a vulture, waiting for me to break under the sheer weight of its presence.

The announcements ended and everyone milled around, returning to their regular eighth-period routine. I gave Vince a peck on the cheek. "I have to do some work in the journalism room."

"See you tonight?" he asked.

"Tonight?"

"A real date. I'll pick you up at seven."

I bit my lip to keep my smile from taking over my face. A thrill went through me, and I felt like this was finally the beginning. I couldn't help but give him another kiss in response.

"Sounds great," I said as I left.

Logan met me at the doors.

"What'd you think?" he asked. He leaned against the wall, all swagger and smiles. My smile disappeared.

"It was great." My voice sounded flat to my own ears, so I kept talking to mask it. I was upset at Elena, but not Logan.

Okay, maybe a little at Logan, too. Was I that easy to forget?

"You definitely got everyone's attention. What was written on the sign?"

"I asked if she'd go to homecoming with me. She said yes."

I didn't say it, but the idea made me nauseous.

"How'd you know the dance?" I asked rather than follow my uncomfortable line of thought.

Logan grinned. "Couple of weeks ago Ron and I were talking. He said show choir was harder than tennis, and of course I disagreed. One thing led to another."

I raised my eyebrows.

"We made a bet." Logan shrugged one shoulder, still smug. "He had ten tries to beat me at tennis, and I had ten hours to learn one of his routines. Guess you know who won the bet."

I laughed. "So what did you get for winning?"

"I told him he owed me something in the future. He just paid off his debt."

"You like doing that, don't you?" I asked. "Holding a debt over people's heads and then cashing in when you see fit."

"Yeah, well, I wouldn't have made him do it. I actually thought about backing out, but Ron wouldn't let me because he's a total show-off. Plus this will get him points with Tania. With you, you couldn't get me out of that soccer game fast enough, so something tells me you secretly wanted to go out with me, too."

Something in my chest hitched, waiting and wishing for him to claim that Elena was just a decoy. Logan didn't have any epiphany, though. He looked at something or someone behind me and within a few seconds, his expression changed. He hiked his bag farther up on his shoulder. That sensation in my chest deflated. "Well, uh, I should go thank Ron for helping me out," he said. "I'll see you around."

He slipped back into the throng of people, and I escaped through the doors. Robyn was waiting for me on the other side, watching Logan as he walked away, but Elena caught up to me before I had taken ten steps. If her face was any indication, I was in for a world of pain.

"I can't believe you," she said. "I know my article was bad, but if you were angry, you should have just told me. You shouldn't have done this."

"What are you talking about?" I said, trying to keep my voice even. With how much practice I was putting in at controlling my emotions, I could probably pass for a robot.

"I know you're behind all this. You have Logan so wrapped around your finger, he'd do anything for you, but making fun of the fact that I'm single is low, even for you. And to do it in front of everyone is even worse. You made me into the bad guy here. If I said no to him, everyone would think I was a jerk, but when I cut things off after only one date, they'll think that anyway. I know Logan is only interested in you, but they don't know that. They don't know he's only pretending so that you can get back at me. How could you?"

My mouth hung open. I couldn't help the anger that was building up like a Mentos put inside a shaken Pepsi. Robyn looked up and down the hallway, perhaps searching for a teacher among all the students. Or maybe she just didn't want witnesses who could connect this to her business and was looking to see if anyone was paying attention. I couldn't be bothered by that, though; I was too angry at what Elena had said.

"Drama queen much?" I said. "First of all, you're just the pot calling the kettle black. You say I should have told you I was angry? Well, speak for yourself. No one forced you to write that article, you know. Don't you try blaming it on Mr. Quince's competition. And secondly, Logan really does like you, not that you deserve it."

Elena laughed, a hard, bitter sound. It wasn't a laugh she'd ever directed at me before, and I took an involuntary step back. How had things gotten so bad between us?

"Don't mock me," she said. "You put him up to this. I saw him give you a thumbs-up after he was done."

I let out a huff of air, but she spoke over me.

"It was bad enough that you had him interrupt our spirit week announcement, but having him pretend to like me is stupid. What are you really hoping to achieve? Did you want to see me fall all over him and then laugh when it was all a joke? Well, too bad, Mia. The joke's on you." She put her hands on her hips. "You know what? I don't care. You play your little game. I'm done."

Then she turned on her heel and began to walk away.

"If that's how you treat friends, then maybe it's for the best," I called after her. I choked out the words, because I already wanted to take them back.

She turned. "Friends? Friends take an interest in my life. They know who I like. They ask how callbacks went. They don't pull stuff like this. And that goes for both of you."

Elena walked off, while I struggled not to cry. I felt like I'd been hit by a bus. The big double-decker kind.

Robyn bit her lip and put an arm across my shoulders.

"Want to get out after school? Do something?" she asked softly. "Or do you want some time to be alone?"

I shook my head but remained silent. When I could trust myself to speak, I asked, "What should we do?"

"I don't know. Coffee shop? Retail therapy? We could shop for homecoming dresses, and you could try on all the sparkly jewelry."

I gave her a wobbly smile. I'd gotten my formal dress with my mom already. But Robyn's parents weren't exactly hands-on, unless her brothers were involved. Maybe a little frivolous shopping was exactly what I needed.

I nodded and Robyn smiled, which immediately loosened the knot in my chest by a fraction. If nothing else, at least I could still make my best friend happy.

If only Elena were so easy to please.

fifteen

The store bell chimed when I opened the door, and a wave of incense hit me, causing me to wrinkle my nose. Why dress shops had to smell like the inside of a wedding bouquet was beyond me. If anything, it made me want to leave the shop faster, before buying the uncomfortable shoes that would promptly be discarded at the side of the dance floor come homecoming night. There weren't many store options in our town, though, so it wasn't like I had much choice.

"Robyn?" I called, walking toward the dressing rooms in the back. She'd texted me a few minutes ago, so I knew she was here already.

"Here!" she called, waving a hand above one of the doors. "What do you think of this one?"

She pulled open the door and emerged in a gorgeous red-satin dress.

"Super cute," I said, motioning for her to turn around. She gave a twirl, and I noticed the oversize red bow in the back. "Perfect for Cupid."

"Right?" She flounced into the main room of the shop to stand in front of the three-way mirror. The door dinged as someone else entered, and I turned to find Logan standing awkwardly in the entryway.

"Robyn," I said, drawing out her name. "What is Logan doing here?"

She glanced past her shoulder and motioned him over. He walked toward us cautiously.

"I think this is the one," Robyn said to us both, swishing the skirt in the mirror. "I'm out."

"But I just got here!" I said.

"And you were going to help me pick out a tux," Logan said. But he didn't look surprised. Was he in on this? Whatever this was? The tux-rental store was right next door to this one, which explained why he was meeting Robyn here.

"I already picked a few out and put your name on them," she said, patting Logan's shoulder. "Mia can help you decide which one looks best."

Oh no I couldn't. Maybe I'd have to spend time with Logan for the journalism competition, but that was where I was drawing the line.

But Robyn was already walking back toward the dressing rooms like the matter was decided. How early had she gotten here to have picked out tuxes for Logan *and* tried on dresses herself? Or had she decided on this dress long ago, and only used shopping as an excuse to bring me and Logan together?

But *why*? She wanted me to work out with Vince. And she'd set Logan up with Elena. That was what Robyn wanted, right? I knew I hadn't spent much quality time with my best friend lately, but it was like I couldn't read her at all anymore.

Robyn closed the door to the dressing room, sequestering herself inside. I refused to look at Logan. Logan, who was casually leaning against the wall, watching me blush and squirm. I fiddled with my purse strap instead of meeting his gaze, wondering if I should tell Vince about this on our date tonight. Then I wondered if that meant I'd already decided to go with Logan to the tux shop.

Robyn emerged a minute later, fully clothed, with dress in hand. She walked directly to the cashier counter without saying anything. I followed, because really, what else was I supposed to do? Hang on her ankles and beg her to stay? I wasn't that desperate. Yet.

She paid for the dress and turned to face Logan and me.

"You'll be fine without me. Just don't let him wear a yellow shirt," she said, directing the last comment at me. "It wouldn't look good with his olive skin."

"I really have some journalism articles I should be—" I said.

"No, you don't," Robyn cut in. "You were going to help me for the next hour, so I know you're free."

One side of Logan's mouth quirked up in a grin, and he shoved his hands deep in his pockets.

I swallowed.

This was dangerous territory. But just because I was with Vince didn't mean I couldn't be friends with other guys. Right? And I needed to stay on Logan's good side to get the better pictures for my articles. So hanging out with him would be in my own best interest.

"Okay," I found myself saying. I'd help him find a tux and be out of there before anything funny could happen. In and out. I tried to catch Robyn's eye to figure out what she meant by putting us together yet again. But Robyn wasn't giving away her secrets.

She left with a wave, and Logan and I awkwardly walked next door, a foot between us the whole time. Logan asked the employee which pieces had been set aside while I wandered the rows of suits, my hand trailing along the fabric. Did Vince have his picked out? Would he wear a tux or a regular suit? I hoped he knew our homecoming was formal. But he hadn't asked me what I'd be wearing so he could coordinate vest colors or anything like that. Did that mean anything?

"I'll be in the first dressing room," Logan said, his breath tickling my ear. I jumped and spun. When had he walked up behind me? I brushed the goose bumps on my arms and took a step back.

"Okay, I'm coming," I said, motioning for him to lead the way.

He raised his eyebrows but otherwise didn't move. "Into my dressing room?"

My cheeks flamed. "Of course not." I cleared my throat. "They have chairs right outside, next to the mirrors. I'll wait there."

He smirked, like maybe he knew the thoughts that had run through my head just a second before. Then he turned and walked back the way he'd come.

I followed slowly, scolding myself the whole while. Before all this mess started, I'd been able to see how Logan's behavior wasn't really flirting. That was just who he was. Like a fish needing water, Logan got his kicks out of seeing me blush.

So how come it affected me so much now? Why couldn't I turn it off?

Logan is just being friendly, I told myself.

I'd like to be friendly *with him*, my traitorous thoughts answered back. I shushed them and focused on putting one foot in front of the other.

I was focusing so hard, I didn't realize we'd already reached the dressing rooms and I'd almost followed Logan inside.

"I was joking earlier," he said, leaning against the door-frame. "But if you really want to come in . . ."

"No!" I blurted, stepping back so fast, I bumped into the wall. "No, I'm good, really. I'll wait here. You go change."

"But don't change too much, right? You like me just the way I am."

I scowled and pushed him into the changing room, closing the door and leaning against it with a silent sigh. Why did boys make everything so difficult? Clutching my purse, I walked to the chairs and sank into one.

Get a grip, I told myself. *What would Vince think?*

That shut me up.

Maybe Robyn had done this as a test of how much I really liked Vince.

If so, I was failing.

I opened the notepad app on my phone and tried to brainstorm article ideas for the paper while Logan changed. How could I make sports more interesting to someone who wasn't interested in them? Someone like me? Because if I could figure out how to do that, I'd double my chances at winning that internship. Mr. Quince had done me a favor when he'd passed Spencer's column to me. If only I could figure out how to exploit it.

The dressing-room door clicked open, and Logan emerged. Shirtless.

"Which one of these should I wear?" he asked, holding out two shirts. I wasn't focusing on that, though, because *hello*, Logan was shirtless!

Did he know what his abs did to girls? I tore my gaze from the muscles in question and looked at the shirts. One was blue, the other green.

"Ummm," I said. Super coherent. That was me.

"Do you know what color dress Elena is wearing?" Logan asked.

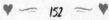

Yes. Elena. Logan was going to homecoming with Elena, and I had no right ogling his abs. Or his biceps. Or the way his pants hung on his hips, leaving just enough to the imagination. Feeling hot all over, I swung my gaze around, looking everywhere but at him.

"Ummm. She told me it was black." Back when we were still talking. That thought brought another pang. "So that means she'll match with any shirt you wear."

"Okay, but which one of these should I wear with these pants?"

The tux was black. It wasn't like either shirt would clash. I had a feeling Logan was doing this simply because he could. Playing with me. Taunting. The thought made me a little mad and gave me courage to stand up, look Logan in the eye, and push a shirt into his rock-hard chest.

"This one," I said, not even noticing which one it was.

Logan smirked, knowing full well he'd won this round. I turned on my heel and marched back to my chair, not turning around until I heard the click of his dressing-room door.

He came out a minute later, fully clothed this time, thankfully.

I let myself eye his frame. It was what I was here for, after all.

"That one's all right," I said, feigning indifference.

"Only all right?" he asked, his dimples in full force. "Guess I need to keep trying, then."

No. He didn't need to keep trying. If he did, he might just

break my resolve once and for all, and that would be a complete and utter disaster, as my pros-and-cons list made clear. The entire school would go back to judging me, Robyn's business would tank, and I would be in a relationship with someone who wasn't serious about anything. Myself included. Plus Robyn would have every reason in the world to hate me, even if her actions today still made absolutely zero sense.

I took a deep breath and let it out. Logan disappeared into his changing room again, and I mentally listed all of Vince's positive characteristics.

I simply needed to get to know Vince better. Give him a chance. I'd gone through all the effort of securing this relationship—but I'd barely given it a shot. This was my chance to learn everything there was to know about Vince, so Robyn couldn't claim anymore that I only liked the idea of him. I straightened my shoulders and sat up in the chair.

I was the one who needed to try harder.

"What are you working on while you wait?" Logan asked, his voice muffled through the door.

"Article ideas for the paper," I answered. "My last sports piece didn't bring in nearly enough page views." Even though I'd clicked refresh on my own computer probably a dozen times. I had to do my part to convince the school that students read it, after all. "Did you think it was okay?"

"I didn't read it."

That wasn't the answer I was expecting.

"I don't read any of the paper. Ever."

"Ever?" I gasped. "I know you said you didn't like the news, but you *never* read the paper? Even ours? You're *on* the newspaper staff."

"Goes against my principles," he said. I could hear the joke in his voice—could picture the way his dimples would deepen and his eyes would glint.

But—he didn't even read my articles?

Obviously, I'd made the right choice. The only choice. Vince did well in school. Vince read the paper.

Logan emerged again, in a different tux and a black shirt. The all-black ensemble suited him so well that I nearly swallowed my gum, and Logan grinned. But a relationship wasn't all about butterflies and sparks. It needed something more to really last, and Vince had that kind of commitment. I just had to prove it.

"So this one then?" he asked, and I wondered why I bothered pretending. "Think Elena will like it?"

Right. Logan was interested in Elena now, which meant he really. Was. Not. Flirting. With. Me.

If he did like me, he'd have read my articles. Did he read Elena's? I couldn't bring myself to ask the question.

"Yes," I said as calmly as I could muster. "Elena will love it." If my voice sounded a little flat, no one could blame me. I picked up my purse and slung it over my shoulder. "Sorry, I have to go." *Have to go get my head on straight* was more like it.

Logan looked a little surprised but quickly masked his expression, so I wondered whether I'd imagined it.

"I have to get ready for my date." It was more a reminder for myself than for Logan, but he nodded anyway.

I left uneasy, hating that I felt so unsettled when everything was supposed to be neatly lined up like dominoes. Dominoes that might come crashing down with just a single push.

sixteen

My parents didn't like me going out on school nights, which meant that convincing them I'd finished all my homework and could be trusted to return by curfew took a full half hour. That was thirty minutes of my life I'd never get back. Dad caved as soon as I passed him a pack of Oreos under the table, but my mom was another story entirely. Eventually, I made it out the door.

Vince and I pulled into the rec center parking lot, and I checked my hair in the mirror of the visor. Wednesday was discount night for all Athens High students, so I'd probably—no, definitely—run into a lot of my classmates tonight. I didn't need to give them any ammunition by not looking my best.

"Ready?" Vince asked, taking the keys from the ignition. My nerves were jangling twice as much as the keys, and I gave Vince a shaky smile.

"I guess?"

We walked through the doors, and I was immediately assaulted by the bright lights and sounds of people talking over one another. Oh, and the smell of too many teenagers in one common room. That was lovely.

"What first?" Vince asked. "Pool? Shuffleboard? Ping-Pong? No, wait, you're a bowling kind of girl, aren't you?" He gestured to the separate rooms in turn, ending with the bowling lanes down the hall.

"Tempting, but I definitely need some food first before I publicly embarrass myself," I said. Vince laughed like he thought I was joking.

Thankfully, he brought me over to the concession line anyway.

So far, the best part about tonight was that no one was giving me the cold shoulder. When Vince offered to pay for my popcorn and bottled water, a girl in line behind us actually shot me an envious look. Somehow that felt better than a smile.

Phase one—get Vince to go out with me—was a success. Phase two—get to know each other so we could recognize our soul-mate potential—oh, it was happening. I knew we were both planners; after all, he already had much of his future plotted out. But besides our organized nature and overachiever attitudes, we had to have something else in common.

"So, Vince," I said, switching the water bottle to my other hand and taking a piece of popcorn from the tub he held. "I was wondering—"

"Hey, look, there's Elena," he said, pulling me by the hand down the hall to the entrance of the bowling alley, where Elena stood with a few of her theater friends. Well, this was just peachy. Robyn thought they'd be a great match, so this boded well. Not. Plus Elena was pretty much the last person I wanted to talk to right now. Or ever.

"I think I'll go to the bathroom before we start any games," I said, freeing my hand from his.

Vince stopped. "I thought you guys made up," he said. "She told me she apologized for the article."

"She did," I said. "We're just not really talking to each other right now." I'd never expected to be on the receiving end of one of her freeze-outs, and the thought made me crumble inside. Would we ever bounce back? I wanted the fun Elena again, the one who played pranks and was overly dramatic. Just not dramatic in this way.

"Mia." He gave me a look. His expression made it obvious that he totally didn't see things like I did.

How come *this* couldn't be something we shared in common?

"Hey, she's not exactly blameless here," I said, taking a step back. Vince came closer and placed a hand on my arm.

"I know," he said. "I didn't mean it like that. Look, you go to the bathroom and I'll say hi to Elena. Want to bowl first? I'll go find an open group."

I beamed up at him gratefully. "You're the best," I said, and placed a kiss on his cheek. He turned his head to give me a kiss on the lips. Then he dropped the hand from my face to give me a small push in the direction of the bathrooms.

Vince continued down the hall and I ducked behind a corner where I could watch his interaction with Elena. She saw Vince and smiled, reminding me of all the times we'd joked together. When was the last time we'd even acknowledged each other? It wasn't like we'd been best friends before, but she was one of the only friends I had. I wasn't the most extroverted person around. Watching them talk made my stomach feel hollow, and I turned away.

I took my time in the bathroom, washing my hands until they were pink. When I couldn't put it off any longer, I made my way back toward the bowling lanes, expecting Vince to have gone inside and found an open spot. He hadn't. He and Elena were still talking off to the side of the entrance, though her friends had left to find seats at an open lane. My footsteps slowed and I desperately looked around for something that might save me from another confrontation with my former friend. If we actually talked, I might say things I'd later regret. Right now I needed to know we still had hope.

Elena's eyes met mine and her jaw clenched. By the time I made it to Vince's side, I was pretty sure she'd need dental work from how much she was grinding her teeth.

"Hi, Elena," I said, trying to sound indifferent. "What a nice surprise."

She tossed her hair over her shoulder.

"Yes, well, not much of a surprise, really," she said. "Athens

High discount nights are my favorite. Vince knows that. We almost always run into each other here."

Was she trying to make me jealous? Well, it wasn't going to work. I put my arm through Vince's and leaned against him.

"That's nice," I said. "Vince, maybe we should go in."

"Okay," he said, turning around and searching the groups with his eyes, taking a few steps. Elena trailed after us.

The bowling section was in a separate room from the rest of the rec center, with only three lanes and a few seats at each ball return. In the dim light, I could see Elena's friends waving her over, and I suppressed a groan. The only two empty seats for any games were with her group.

By the time we slid into our seats, though, I had a hard time holding back my smile. I was Vince's girlfriend. Here we were, hanging out with his friends as if it was normal for someone like Vince to be out with someone like me. Our fingers touched while reaching for popcorn, and my smile doubled in size.

I didn't pay much attention to the game. My mind was a little preoccupied with Vince's arm muscles. Well, that and wondering how on earth I would salvage my friendship with Elena. Because with each silent glare she sent my way, the temperature in the room dropped by twenty degrees.

When Elena finished her turn, she sat back down and I cleared my throat.

"So," I said, accidentally spilling a little water when I squeezed the bottle too hard. Talking to Elena didn't used to be difficult. But now I could feel the panic building in my chest like a balloon on the edge of bursting. Why did I feel like each word coming out of my mouth was a potential bomb? "How were callbacks?" I set the water aside and wiped my hands on my jeans.

She rolled her eyes but quickly schooled her expression when Vince looked her way. "Good, I guess. I got the part I wanted."

"That's great," I said, pulling the tub of popcorn closer. Maybe if I had something to do with my hands, this conversation wouldn't make me want to hide under the table for eternity. "What part is that again?"

"The low-class wannabe who pretends to be your friend but is too busy stabbing your back to notice no one likes her."

I inhaled sharply—and promptly started choking on a piece of popcorn. My coughing seemed magnified in the silence surrounding Elena's comment. It wasn't the pretty kind of cough, either. It was the *holy-crap-I'm-going-to-die-by-popcorn* kind of cough.

Vince removed his hand from my leg and started thumping my back. People across the bowling alley turned to see what all the fuss was all about. I felt the sharp edges of the kernel scraping my throat as it debated whether to go up or down. Elena gave me a dirty look before turning back to her other friends. Good to know my imminent death meant so much to her.

In fact, everyone ignored me. Even once my coughing was over, they turned to one another like I didn't exist. Like Elena hadn't just slapped me with her words. No one came to my defense. I was the outsider, the person who threatened their social standing with my mere existence as Vince's girlfriend. I looked over at him to see if my knight in shining armor would come to my rescue. But Vince was busy staring at his shoes.

I picked my bag up off the floor and stood up. I'd had such high hopes for tonight. Maybe it was my fault for expecting too much.

My bag shook in my arms, and I tried to catch Vince's eye. When he didn't look up, I felt my anger go up a notch, like a hook in my heart I couldn't remove. I didn't even wait to make sure Vince would follow. I just walked toward the exit as fast as possible.

Vince caught up to me when I was nearly at the front doors of the rec center.

"You didn't even try to defend me," I said, pushing open the doors with more force than was necessary. Maybe my next article would be about high school cliques. If I included enough of them, I could get everyone to read it. And then they'd all find out how horrible Elena's group was.

"There wasn't any time to." He reached out to touch me on the arm, but I brushed him off. The crisp evening air felt good on my overheated skin, and I took a step away.

"I'm sorry, Mia." He took my hand, closing the distance. "I should have said something. Elena's not usually like that. You know," he said, weaving his fingers through mine, "for what it's worth, she really did get the part of the shrew."

Against my will, a small chuckle escaped. It was like the part was made for her. Of course, right after I thought that, I felt a flash of guilt. If Elena and I had any chance at making things right, I needed to stop being so critical of her every move.

We walked the rest of the way to the car in silence. He opened the door for me, and I slid into the seat. He put an arm at the top of the open door and leaned on the frame, his eyes focused on something in the distance.

"Mia, do you even like me?" he asked.

I looked up in surprise. "What?"

"You say you're in this relationship, but it doesn't feel like it." His brows were furrowed, his voice low. "Whenever we're in public, you act so distant. I can't tell what you're thinking. I mean, I practically serenaded you at a soccer game, for crying out loud, and you haven't even told anyone we're a couple." He shook his head. "Are you sure this is what you want? I'm giving it my all, but you . . ."

I stepped out of the car, but Vince didn't back up, so we were pressed next to each other in the small space between the open door and the car. If he needed some kind of public declaration, then I'd do it when we were around our classmates, but I needed to at least make things better now. He was so right. I'd been acting without thinking.

I put my hands on his chest. How lucky was I to have a completely honest and open boyfriend, even when I kept everything from him? Of course, even now, there was a traitorous corner of my brain that whispered of someone else I knew with strong chest muscles, and I let out a shaky breath.

But then my eyes connected with Vince's again, and I saw the hurt there. Stretching up on my tiptoes, I softly kissed him. He reciprocated hesitantly at first, before shifting our bodies so we pushed up against the side of the car. When he deepened the kiss, I felt a thrill race from my fingers to my toes.

I was doing the right thing. Vince's kiss convinced me of that. He was suffering right now, but I was going to find a way to make everything better. Vince was all in, and it was time for me to get off the fence. I mean, look at how quickly Logan had moved on to Elena. He obviously wasn't boyfriend potential.

I kissed Vince and let myself enjoy it. He really was a good kisser. I thought of all the reasons I'd matched us together in the first place, and this time, I pushed the regret to the back of my mind. I locked it away and vowed not to let it in again. I told myself I could be happy in this relationship.

After all the lies I'd told myself that week, it wasn't hard to add another to the list.

seventeen

Somehow Vince convinced me to go on a double date on Thursday night.

With Elena and Logan.

I wasn't sure how it happened, but I was guessing it had something to do with Vince's blue puppy-dog eyes and how I felt guilty about everything. Vince could have asked me to shave my head and I probably would have said yes. I'd written another article about soccer last night after our date, and watching YouTube clips of his games only made me like him more. He was so dedicated and focused—willing to put in the work and make sacrifices. It was a spark of hope. Because it meant our relationship was brimming with possibilities.

Still. This double date was not good. And how had he convinced Elena?

Maybe he'd blackmailed her. Or maybe Robyn was right,

and Elena really did like Vince. It would certainly explain some of her hostility toward me, even if she did claim there was nothing between them.

I worried about it the entire way to the mini-golf place and nonstop while we played the first few holes. I couldn't help but wonder if there was something going on between them.

That thought made my head hurt, so instead I focused on hitting the ball into the hole. Mini-golf was not my forte. I was at least eight strokes behind everyone else—a fact that Logan seemed to get immense satisfaction from.

"You're not perfect at everything, then. That's good to know," he said into my ear.

The way his breath tickled my neck sent shivers down my arms as I tried to hit the stupid ball. All night he'd gone back to his regular taunting, taking pictures he claimed were for the yearbook, when really he was probably planning to blackmail us with them when this date was over.

My ball went wide, bouncing off the wall and sliding down the fake grass until it finally stopped a good two feet from the hole.

"That's okay, babe; you'll get it next time."

Vince didn't seem to notice how his comment irked everyone in our group, me most of all, Elena for who knew what reason, and Logan because Vince was now standing right in front of his shot. Vince moved, Logan took his turn, and then Elena came to the front of the hole.

She looked back at Logan, who was now leaning casually

against the fake towering boulders, his arms crossed against his chest. Her gaze ping-ponged to Vince, who was standing next to me, one arm now around my waist. She rested her weight on her golf club, cocking her hip to the side.

"You," she said, pointing to Logan. He stepped away from the boulder, coming to her side with eyebrows raised.

"Yes?"

"You asked me to homecoming."

"Yes." Logan seemed confused by this line of questioning. As was I. Especially when Elena whipped around to face me.

"And you say he really does like me."

I looked across at Logan, who shrugged, like he had no more idea what this was all about than I did.

"Yes," I said. Talking with Elena this whole night had been like scraping nails along a chalkboard. Unfortunately, she and Vince seemed like a package deal, so even if I hadn't been wanting to patch things up between us, I'd have to learn to play nice. Still, monosyllabic words were about all I could muster. Maybe, with enough time, I could remember the fun side of Elena, the side I missed more than anything, but right now I could barely even smile.

"Okay." Elena was nodding to herself. She looked again at Vince, her expression unreadable. Then she turned to face Logan directly. "Then prove it."

His eyebrows scrunched together as he thought about her words. "H-how?"

Then Elena, true to her unpredictable nature, did the one thing I'd never expected her to do.

Elena kissed Logan.

It was silent all around us—except for the screaming going on in my head.

I didn't like this.

Not. One. Bit.

Fire coursed through my veins, every nerve ending in my body shouting for me to take Elena by her shoulders and do *something*. I wasn't sure what. Punch her? Gouge her eyes out? Compose awful poetry, rhyming her name with really despicable synonyms? I wanted to do all those things and then some. Not because of all the horrible things Elena had done to me, but because she was kissing Logan. I wanted to force Elena and Logan apart and shove her into the mini-golf pond to my left. The water smelled about as awful as I felt. She'd probably contract some deadly disease, and it'd serve her right. The putrid, green water might even do permanent damage to her hair. Her hair that she was always so proud of. I wanted to set fire to that hair.

I wanted to eat all the ice cream in the world. I wanted to cry big, fat, ugly tears.

But I didn't. Instead I stood there, frozen. We all did, each of us waiting for the kiss to end. Vince still clutched my waist. Logan hadn't moved, apparently too surprised to act in any way.

I was surprised myself. At my own reaction. I never would have suspected the jealousy to take over as completely as it had. Sure, I knew Logan had gotten under my skin. I knew he affected me and I liked him. But still? Even after committing myself to Vince, I couldn't get my heart to agree with my head. I'd thought that eventually Vince would replace Logan and I could merrily go on my way. I hadn't thought Logan would claim that part of my heart only to never give it back. I never thought a pros-and-cons list could lie.

I tried to imagine my reaction if Vince had been the one Elena kissed.

Nothing.

I literally felt nothing. If Elena kissed Vince, I didn't think I'd care. And that thought turned my world on its axis. Because I did care that she was kissing Logan. I cared a whole lot. This was the straw that broke my back, and I couldn't shoulder the weight.

She finally ended the kiss, relaxing back onto her heels.

Logan looked at me. Elena looked at Vince. I looked at Logan. Vince looked at Elena. It was like one of those slow-motion videos. I could almost imagine the view panning out, then zooming in on each of our faces as we waited for someone to speak first.

"Well, uh . . ." Logan brought his hand to the back of his neck. "I certainly wasn't expecting that."

That made two of us. Three if you counted Vince, because I was pretty sure he was just as shocked, given the fact that his grip on my waist had tightened to an uncomfortable level.

I was so, so incredibly stupid. I'd been fighting a losing battle all along, so desperate for . . . what? Validation? A picture-perfect homecoming date that I could brag about ten years from now? What did any of that matter?

Plotting out my future didn't matter if I wasn't happy in it. What use were plans A, B, and C if each of them were equally awful? And worst of all, I had dragged everyone else down with me. *Stupid Mia. Poor, blind, stupid Mia.* I'd tried pretending my feelings for Logan were superficial, but it wasn't until I saw him kissing someone else that I was finally able to admit they weren't going away anytime soon. No matter how much I tried to put someone else in his place.

"That was interesting," Elena said, crossing her arms.

It was? What did that mean?

"Maybe I'll write about this in my next gossip article," Elena said. I swallowed. That sounded foreboding. I needed to change the subject. Fast.

"Maybe we should move to the next hole?" I said. If we kept moving, maybe I could pretend like the last five minutes hadn't happened. There was only one hole left and then I could go home, crawl beneath my covers, and bawl my eyes out. Earlier we'd discussed going out for dessert, but there was no way that was happening now. Every additional second was torture. Sitting in a mostly empty diner, quietly eating pie and pretending like I didn't want the guy on the opposite side of the table, well, that didn't seem like a good time to me.

"Yes, one hole left," Vince said, his voice strained.

Maybe all of us were dying to get through this evening. Or maybe I was the only one. Either way, it was obvious my feelings for Logan weren't dead. Not by a long shot.

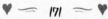

eighteen

I needed to ask Robyn for advice. But I couldn't work up the guts until Friday afternoon, when the weekend was staring me in the face with all its loneliness. It wasn't like I was going to hang out with Elena, and Vince was out of town with away games all weekend. Logan was probably busy planning a candlelit dinner with my frenemy, so I finally broke down and asked Robyn if she was busy. An hour later I was waiting for her, pacing outside the coffee shop like I'd already had one too many cappuccinos.

"Hey there, stranger," a voice said behind me. I turned and Robyn slung an arm around me, leading me inside. Once there, she dropped her purse onto a booth seat, scooting in until she was leaning against the wall, and stuck her feet out in front of her.

"Make yourself comfortable," I said. Nope, my voice wasn't shaking. Not. One. Bit.

"How's my bestie? The journalism competition? I feel like it's been forever since we've chatted. How's Vince?" She sounded so happy and oblivious to all the pain I'd been creating. I hated to burst her bubble.

"He's fine. I'm still behind the comics in the competition, and I can't think of an original idea to save my life." Yeah, like I didn't have enough stress to go around. "How's your matchmaking biz?"

I held my breath while waiting for her answer, because that would determine my next move. Was she in a good mood? A bad one? If I told her I had feelings for Logan, would she hate me forever? Anxiety wormed its way into my stomach, flipping it around like a puppy's chew toy. Telling Robyn might end badly. So very badly.

My heartbeat could probably rival that of a humming-bird, and I couldn't seem to take in a full breath. Everything else had crashed and burned—I couldn't afford to lose Robyn, too. If I played my cards wrong, she might want nothing to do with me. I'd have to live out the rest of my high school life as a complete social outcast. I'd probably become a hermit who ate lunch in a bathroom stall.

"It is what it is," she said, picking up some sugar packets and starting to build a house with them.

What did that mean? It was like she was being vague on purpose. Robyn knew me too well, though, which meant she probably already knew where this conversation was going.

"What'd you think of Logan's flash mob?" Robyn placed another packet carefully, not looking me in the eye. Yep, she was definitely leading this conversation somewhere. I'd never

felt so out of touch with my best friend before. We hadn't really talked since Logan asked Elena to homecoming. And the two minutes we'd gone dress shopping hadn't counted. Lately I'd been focusing so much on my next article, and Robyn had mysterious journalism work, so we'd gone our separate ways the past few days. I sighed as I sat down, my knee hitting the table and causing Robyn's sugar packet tower to fall. She scowled and began again.

"It was . . . great?" Lie. But I was trying to feel her out, see where she stood.

Robyn raised one eyebrow.

"Yes. Very . . . educational." Another lie. Why was it so hard to tell Robyn the truth? It was what I'd come here to do, but admitting I was wrong somehow tasted sour. Like saying everything I'd ever stood for was false. I put my head down on my arms, muffling my next confession. "Okay, it was torture. You happy?"

"You mean you've learned your lesson?" She practically purred with satisfaction. I raised my head to give her a dirty look.

"You don't have to sound so happy about it."

"I'm not happy you're upset. I'm simply glad you can see my side now. Logan's side. Elena's. Not just your own."

Logan's side—that was easy. Elena's? That was a whole lot harder. All I knew was that every time I faced her, I was in foreign territory. Our conversations were pinched and I was unsure of my own footing, stumbling around as I tried to regain some sense of normalcy. But if she was being genuine, if she really felt like all this was my fault and I'd orchestrated Logan liking her. . . . well, that would be pretty awful. I could give her that much. How would I react if I thought my friend had done that to me? Especially if I thought she'd stolen the guy I liked only to throw it in my face?

"I get it," I said. "Messing with people's hearts is a serious business. I already feel terrible. You don't have to make it worse."

Robyn set the remaining sugar packets aside.

"So you're finally willing to admit you were wrong?"

"About so many things."

"Repeat after me," she said. "I, Mia, hereby proclaim that Robyn is always right. And she is the most beautiful, most talented, most supremely perfect person ever."

I slugged her in the arm, and she pretended to be hurt. She took a deep breath and looked me in the eye.

"So what are you going to do about it?"

My shoulders slumped. "I have no idea. Help me."

She pursed her lips. "You're the one who got yourself into this mess. You have to get yourself out of it."

"Please, I'm begging you. Tell me what I should do. Nothing makes sense. Vince and I aren't working, Logan is chasing after Elena, and I'm pretty sure all this stress is giving me acne." I pointed to my forehead for emphasis.

"Well, we can't have that, now can we?" She cracked a smile, and I knew I was forgiven. "All right, I'll give you my advice. But you have to promise you won't hurt my business any more than you already have. I'm behind almost a whole month in saving for my car. I tried telling people that my contract only guarantees one date and that sometimes things don't work out, but that doesn't make them more likely to entrust me with their love lives. Whatever you do, leave my business out of it, and make sure people know you're acting on your own."

I nodded, and Robyn stuck out her hand for me to shake. "Deal."

"Okay, first step: Forget about Vince. Entirely." She pointed a finger at me, like a warning. "Sorry, Mia, I know you're worried about homecoming, and I hate to be the one to break it to you, but this perfect idea you have in your head just isn't going to happen. You wanted honesty, right?"

It was sweet she'd try to spare my feelings, but it wasn't anything I hadn't already admitted to myself.

"Yeah, yeah, I get it. He's out of my league, anyway." I was tired of making it work when it so obviously wasn't. The part I hated most was that it was my fault for pushing an agenda that no one agreed with. Now, apparently, not even me. Could I be more awful?

"As your best friend, I hate to disagree with you, but I'm going to have to in this case. I know you, Mia. You're smart and talented, and sure, you sometimes make a fool of yourself, but your heart is in the right place. You care about your friends, and you always try to do the right thing. If Vince can't see all that, then that's his loss and you're the one who's out of his league."

I smiled. "I'd hug you if you weren't across the table."

One half of her mouth quirked up in a grin.

"Okay, so you need to set Vince free. That's step one. Step two: You need to get comfortable with the idea that Vince and Elena are totally meant to be together. I know you aren't exactly supportive of that idea, but it's going to happen, so you have to get on board."

"Done."

She looked skeptical.

"No, really," I said. "I should have seen all the signs earlier. It certainly explains . . . things. Like Elena's reaction when she learned I'd blown off Vince to go to the Pier with Logan. Or how Vince acted around Elena at the bowling alley while I hid in the bathroom. And his strange insistence that I forgive her for the article she wrote. Or the fact that she was the first person he confided in when he worried that I'd kissed Logan in the janitor's closet, leading her to write that piece. This whole time, he's been more interested in her than me, and I was just too caught up to see it." I paused. "That doesn't mean I've totally forgiven Elena, but that's not Vince's fault."

Robyn nodded. "Good."

"But why would he submit an application to you if he already had feelings for Elena?" I asked. "That's the part I don't get."

Robyn leaned back and played with a sugar packet. "Elena submitted an application, too. The day before Vince. My guess is that Vince found out and hurried to get his in."

"You mean he was hoping to be matched with Elena all along."

She nodded.

"But why would Elena submit an application in the first place? She could get any guy she wanted without having someone else set it up. And she told me about a gazillion times that she and Vince were only friends."

"You mean like how you kept telling me you weren't interested in Logan?" Robyn smirked, and I scowled. "Elena's more your friend than mine, but sometimes it's like you don't know her at all." Robyn put the packet down and leaned over on her elbows. "Elena may act super confident, but it's scary to sacrifice a friendship when there's no guarantee a relationship will work. If, however, she could blame the match on someone else . . ." Robyn spread her hands in explanation. "They could go back to friends, and no one would care if things didn't work out."

"Hmm." I stood up and pretended to look at the coffee-shop menu board while I contemplated everything Robyn had said. "But why go through the work of submitting an application? I mean, she could have just asked you."

"Who knows? I'm guessing it's because a few of her friends submitted applications around the same time. Girls' night?" Robyn shrugged. "Or maybe she did it this way simply for the thrill." She got up out of the booth, grabbing her purse. "I think I want a cookie or muffin or something. You?"

I shook my head.

Robyn walked over to the cashier to order while I sat back down.

I did want to see Elena's side of things. Really. All this

stuff between us churned my stomach. Most of the time, we evened each other out—me with my lists, her with her crazy (but crazy-fun) impulsiveness. I just couldn't understand why she'd act this way when it wasn't like it was exactly logical.

Then again, logical thinking had put me in this mess, and if I'd listened to my heart the way Robyn had suggested, maybe I wouldn't be all twisted up inside.

Robyn came back with a brownie and sat down.

"Now, about Logan," she said, picking up her fork. "What's your plan there?" She wiggled her eyebrows.

I sighed, reached over, and stole a chunk of her brownie. She swatted my hand away.

"Get your own. And that statement applies to boys as well as food. It's time you stop chasing after Vince and went after the guy who would actually make you happy. Step three: Win back Logan."

She made it sound so easy. But Logan had already moved on. To Elena.

I scowled and swiped another bite. This time Robyn ignored it, perhaps sensing my need for comfort food.

"But what do I *do*?" I said, dropping my head into my arms on the table. "I can't compete with Elena. Even if she likes Vince, Logan is still chasing after her."

"Show him you're serious!" She thumped the table, and I lifted my head. "Come on and grow a spine already, you jellyfish. You think he likes being your second choice? Show him you're a girl with feelings, and maybe he'll treat you like one."

She leaned close, so her face was only inches from mine. "Tell him the truth."

Four little words that struck such fear into my heart. Still, I nodded, resolve coursing through my veins. I needed to fix this. I needed to get Logan back.

"Just remember not to hurt my business any more while you're at it. You're like a bull in a china shop."

I took a deep breath. "I can do this," I said, more for my benefit than hers. But Robyn must have agreed, because she smiled, popping the last of her brownie into her mouth.

It wasn't much of a plan, but it was a plan. It was something I could actually *do*, rather than sit back and wait.

It was my turn to woo Logan.

nineteen

I didn't waste any time putting my plan in motion. Step one: Free Vince. I called him on my way home from the coffee shop, asking him to meet me at the little diner down the street from my house. I didn't need my parents hovering over this conversation.

It was starting to drizzle when I pulled into the lot and put the car in park. My palms were sweaty against the steering wheel, and I tried to convince myself I was doing the right thing. Would he hate me forever?

I killed the engine and opened the door, pulling up my hood as I walked in the rain. The hostess looked up when I entered, but before she could offer me a seat, I pointed to Vince and went to join him.

"Hey." He smiled, but I could tell it was a little forced—not the true smile he used whenever Elena walked into the room.

"Hey yourself." I sat on the opposite side of the booth, using the table as a buffer between us. Might as well dive in. "So I have a confession."

Judging from the way he drew in a breath, Vince seemed to know what was coming. Or he was nervous about what I would say.

"Can I say something first?" He shifted on his seat, clearly uncomfortable.

"Sure."

He waited a full twenty seconds before starting to talk again. "Maybe we were better as just friends." His words came out in a rush, like he was making up for all the time he'd been silent. I looked around our empty table. Vince hadn't ordered a drink or anything, which meant maybe he was hoping for the same quick escape as me.

"Vince," I said, shaking my head. "We were never really friends before."

"Right," he said. "What I mean is, I don't really think this is going to work." He was still talking too fast. "You feel it, too, don't you? I mean, we just don't make sense."

"No worries. I get it, and I feel the same way. That's actually what I wanted to talk to you about, too."

His eyebrows shot up to his hairline. Maybe he wasn't used to girls breaking up with him. What was I thinking—of course he wasn't. He was Vince Demetrius. Star soccer player and all-around good-guy.

The question was, did I have to confess to hacking Robyn's email?

If the twisting in my gut was any indication, I did. Or else face the wrath of Robyn. She'd made me promise not to do any more damage to her business, and I had a feeling that meant I couldn't let her take the fall for this.

"But there's more," I said, swallowing. "Remember that matchmaking application you sent to Robyn?"

Vince frowned, clearly confused that I knew about the application. I pushed forward before I could chicken out.

"I was the one who responded to your email. Robyn wanted to match you up with Elena, and I went behind her back to set you up with me instead."

There. I'd sealed my fate. I held my breath while I waited for his response. His eyebrows furrowed, but it took him a long time—much too long—to respond.

He shook his head. "Elena? She was really going to match me with Elena?"

I didn't know why he acted so surprised. Like Elena was the one out of *his* league. Well, if I were being honest with myself, I probably would have said she was, back when we were on better terms. Even if things weren't so hot between me and her right now, Vince had better treat her right if he knew what was good for him.

"I know you like her, too. It's okay to admit it."

"'Too'? As in she likes me back? You're sure?"

I didn't know how this conversation had veered left so quickly, but if the alternative was Vince's anger, I'd take it.

"Uh, you think?" I chuckled.

Vince grinned, then seemed to think better of it, frowned, and placed his hands firmly on the edge of the table.

"But I can't believe you did that." He cleared his throat, his voice suddenly tight. "I mean, didn't you even think about how that messed with my life? How was I supposed to feel? That . . . that was a pretty sucky thing to do, Mia."

I held a breath, then slowly released it.

"I know that," I said. "Now." My leg bounced nervously under the table. "At the time, I really liked you and I just thought about homecoming, but that's no excuse. I'm really sorry. Things got out of control."

He nodded slowly. "Maybe you had good intentions." He ran a hand through his hair. "But I still think it's for the best if we kind of . . . avoid each other for a while."

I hastily nodded. Avoiding each other was preferable to Vince publicly denouncing me or shaming me on social media. Not that he really would have done any of those things, but it was still the best-case scenario here. At least this way Elena would see I wasn't chasing after Vince anymore, and maybe she wouldn't burn me at the stake in her gossip column. Hopefully. Maybe she wasn't in the competition anymore, but she still wrote for the paper.

"Right. So, just to be clear, we're breaking up, right?" His voice finally sounded normal. "You're not going to egg my house if I ask Elena to homecoming or anything?"

"Nope. No hard feelings. It's mutual, I promise." After everything else I'd done, the least I could do now was bow out graciously.

He let out a long breath. I expected to feel some disappointment—I'd been crushing on Vince pretty hard, after all. But . . . nothing. Not one bit of regret. Just happiness. Even with the journalism competition hanging over my head, I felt lighter than I had all week.

At least, I did for a few seconds. Then I remembered that Logan still had feelings for Elena and it was up to me to change his mind, or rather, his heart.

"Good luck, Vince." I leaned over and placed a quick kiss on his cheek, standing up as I did so. "Sorry I messed everything up."

Vince looked up at me in the dim lighting of the restaurant. "It wasn't all bad," he said. "It was fun getting to know you."

"You, too," I said. Then I walked away.

Step two: Get on board with Vince and Elena as a couple. That was the easiest of Robyn's steps. It was the third one, telling Logan the truth, that made me hesitate as I buckled my seat belt. I turned the keys and checked the time on the dash. Eight thirty. It wasn't too late yet.

I passed the park where Logan and I had taken our walk. Then I pulled into his driveway, stopped the car, and checked my hair in the rearview mirror.

I took a few deep breaths, then walked to the door and rang the bell before I could change my mind.

Sadie answered, but this time, she wasn't smiling.

"Mia. Nice to see you." Her attitude was cold, but I deserved it.

"Look, Sadie, I'm sorry about how things worked out with your brother." I had prepared what I wanted to say to Logan, but I hadn't prepared for Sadie. Hopefully she was the forgiving type. "I know you think everything is my fault, but I promise I'm trying to do the right thing here."

"Yeah? And just what is it you are trying to do?" she asked.

Good question.

"I'd really like to talk to Logan," I said.

She smirked. "Maybe you should go talk to Vince. He's your boyfriend, isn't he?"

"Vince and I broke up," I said. Her face scrunched as she considered my words, but she didn't look any more forgiving.

"Sorry, I guess," she said. It sounded forced.

"Thanks. Look, is Logan around? I really need to explain a few things to him."

"Yeah."

"Can I talk to him?" Seriously. Could Sadie make this more difficult?

She looked up at the sky and paused, like she wasn't sure what to say. Eventually, she shrugged. "I'll let him decide that," she said.

Then she closed the door in my face.

"What?" I said aloud.

Great, now I was talking to a door. I didn't know if she was going to get Logan or if that had been her not-so-polite way of telling me to go away and leave her family in peace. Was I supposed to wait? I shifted my weight from one leg to the other while I considered my options. Knocking again would make me seem desperate. Leaving would probably be my best bet, but then I wouldn't get to talk to Logan. I did still have a sports piece to write for the competition, and those articles hadn't been coming easy, what with everything else going on.

It was getting cold, so I stuck my hands in my jacket pockets and turned to go back to my car. The rain had stopped, leaving a clear sky filled with stars. Off to my right, I heard a sound and made a girly squeak. I might have also jumped a foot in the air, but I wasn't fessing up to it.

The porch light was still on, and because of it, I could see what had caused the sound. An enormous tree stood next to the house, and from it, a rope ladder had dropped down. Peering into the branches, I saw a small tree house tucked among the leaves.

When nothing else happened, I wiped my shaking hands on my jeans and started climbing the ladder. When I made it to the top, I found Logan stretched out on his back on the wooden platform surrounding the little house, looking at the stars.

The night air was heavy on my skin as I watched Logan for some sign of his mood. If anything, he looked pensive. His hands were behind his head, and he didn't look at me as I crossed to where he was and lay down beside him, mimicking his pose. There wasn't much room between the railing and the outside wall of the tree house, but I was careful not to touch him. I felt the distance stretch between us as I considered what to say. It should be something insightful. Something full of meaning and purpose.

"Hey," I said after a beat of silence. It was the best I could do.

"Hey," he said, still looking at the stars.

"Whatcha doing?" I asked.

"Thinking." He was silent for a bit before continuing. "I used to come here after my dad died. Whenever I needed some space. Mom and Sadie kind of learned to leave me alone." He paused. "You know, I haven't come up here in months."

Guilt hit me again, like a wave. It seemed to be my constant companion these days.

"So what are you thinking about now?" I asked, hoping that maybe this time it wasn't my fault, but feeling deep in my gut like maybe it was. One more thing to add to the list.

"My mom is out on a date tonight. Her first one since my dad died."

Oh. That wasn't what I was expecting.

"I want her to be happy, you know?" Logan said. "And I know that my mom hasn't forgotten my dad or anything like that. But a part of me feels, I don't know. Like, betrayed or something." He paused. "I know it doesn't make sense."

"No, it does," I said, scooting a little closer.

"Do you want to know why I never follow the news or read the school paper?" he asked. His voice was soft, so low I could barely hear him. I scooted even closer.

"Yes."

He turned his face toward me, the shadows dancing across his cheekbones.

"I guess I just hate bad news. Maybe it's because of my dad, I don't know. But it's like I get all anxious and feel like something horrible is bound to happen." His shoulders moved up and down with his heavy sigh.

"And newspapers thrive on that kind of crap. So I don't read them. It's a stupid reason, I know."

"I don't think it's stupid. It makes perfect sense to me." There was enough bad in the world; we didn't need to dwell on it. And Logan had seen his fair share of bad. He couldn't help but blow things out of proportion in his mind. "I'm glad you told me, and I'm sorry about what you're going through now."

"Thanks." He angled his upper body toward me. "You know, I'm pretty sure Sadie blames you for why I'm up here. She thinks I'm licking my wounds over being rejected or something."

"Yeah, ummm. Sorry, I was going to tell her you liked Elena." I tried not to growl when I said her name. "How . . . how are things going there?"

Logan shifted up to his elbows. "They're not. Elena pretty much wants nothing to do with me." He looked at me when he said it. Then, after a moment, he lay back down and rubbed his forehead in defeat. "Dating sucks. And my mom wants to get back into the dating game? Seriously, why?"

"Maybe she's a glutton for punishment?" I said.

Logan laughed. "Yeah, well, it can't all be bad," he said. "You're happy with Vince, right?"

I took a deep breath. "We broke up."

He was silent for a bit. "I'm sorry," he said. But he was smiling. Why was he smiling?

And why did that cause my pulse to skyrocket?

"Don't be. If I'm being honest, it was never really serious." It was time to come clean and put it all out there. No turning back. "I just liked the idea of him. Things went south pretty quickly. We dated, what? A whole week? That's got to be some kind of record, even for high school." I sat up and crossed my legs beneath me. Logan and I were quiet for a bit. The weight of our conversation pressed all around me, crowding out all other thoughts. What I *should* say, what I *wanted* to say—all of it dogpiled until I felt dizzy with anxiety. I lay back down and stared at the stars, taking calming breaths until I felt relatively certain I could talk without my voice catching.

"Despite that major fail, I still believe in relationships. I mean . . . okay, think of your mom. She's gone through pretty much the worst thing that could ever happen. You all have. And she's willing to put herself out there again, rather than be alone. That has to mean something, right? Sure, relationships can suck, but they can also be great."

I felt like I was talking to myself. Logan still hadn't said anything, leaving me to wonder whether he was getting my hint or if I needed to hit him over the head with my feelings.

"I guess I'm a hopeless romantic," I said. I waited for him

to say something—anything—to save me from embarrassing myself, but I could tell he was going to make me say it. The words wanted to stick in my throat, but I forced them out. "I must be. Because I still want the fairy-tale ending. Even when I'm faced with the fact that the only guy I ever truly liked now likes someone else." I tried not to panic, but the words were out now, and nothing could take them back. He had to know I was talking about him.

In the starlight, I searched Logan's face for some kind of response. He lay perfectly still—too still. His face didn't change, and he didn't look over to where I lay. After a silence that was entirely too long, his eyebrows drew together and he propped himself up on one elbow to look at me. But he still didn't say anything.

I mimicked him, propping myself up, bringing us that much closer together. The air buzzed with the electricity between us, but maybe I was the only one affected.

"Should I go? I don't want to take up all your thinking time." I chewed on my lower lip while I waited for him to speak. I vowed to wait it out this time.

He glanced at my lips and back to my eyes. He leaned slightly forward so we were only inches apart, lying on the tree-house platform with the stars above us. I didn't move.

Then Logan closed the distance between us and placed his lips on mine.

My hands seemed to have a life of their own, and the one that wasn't supporting my weight was around his neck before I could process what was happening.

I forgot where we were. I forgot this might not be the best time. I forgot how to breathe, all because Logan was kissing me. His lips were soft and questioning, and I was leaning into him just as much as he was holding me.

He brought one hand to the back of my neck, and I wanted to stay right there forever. I'd thought Vince had been a good kisser, but this was different on so many levels.

Logan caught my lower lip with his and I felt the rush of adrenaline go all the way to my toes. My free hand found his shoulders, then his chest. I needed to feel him close to me, to feel his nearness and know he wasn't going anywhere. He brought his hand from my neck to my cheek before spreading his fingers into my hair, pulling at something much deeper, closing the distance between us in a way I hadn't experienced before. I was dizzy with his kiss, drunk with the feeling of being needed, wanted.

But after a minute, his kiss became hesitant, like he didn't trust himself. Or maybe me. It was more like a question than an answer, and that fear wormed its way deep into my thoughts, until I didn't know what to feel anymore.

Logan pulled back, dropping his hand from my hair. His eyes searched my face for a long moment. My heartbeat was loud in my ears, but I didn't dare break the silence.

"Sorry," he finally said, turning to look up at the stars. "I didn't think that through."

Sorry? What did that mean? I couldn't answer him, so I stared at the sky, looking for the North Star—something to guide my swirling thoughts. We didn't talk for a minute while I waited for Logan to sort through his emotions.

I tried to reach out my hand to hold his, but he pulled back, leaving me confused. My fingers froze in the empty air, paralyzed by his rejection. What did it mean? Had he just been kissing me out of some need for comfort? Because he was already feeling depressed about his mom? Or did the sinking feeling in my gut mean he still liked Elena? It was a crushing thought, and I suddenly found it hard to breathe.

"Mia, are you sure? Like, really sure?" Logan asked suddenly, turning his head to face me in the dark. "You *just* broke up with Vince. I can't be your rebound."

"You're not," I said quickly. "I'm sure."

Maybe I didn't sound convincing enough, because Logan still looked uncertain. The darkness closed in on me then, and I fought to control my expression. I tried one more time to hold his hand, but he moved his farther away.

So was *that* my answer? I took a deep breath and tried to sound more confident than I really felt in that moment.

"Logan, I broke up with Vince because of *you*. You're not my second choice. But are *you* sure?" Maybe he really was interested in Elena. Because I'd pushed him away.

"Sometimes I'm not sure about anything."

His answer took all the breath from my lungs, leaving nothing but a few crumbling echoes. I waited, hoping he'd change his mind, but Logan didn't say anything else.

"I should let you think about things," I said finally, sitting up and placing my hands on my knees. He nodded, which was like a knife to my heart.

I stood up on wobbly legs, climbed down the ladder, and walked away, my hands shaking the whole time. With each step, I felt that knife go deeper and deeper. By the time I reached my car, it had gone all the way through, leaving me hollow and numb.

twenty

Monday mornings were, by their very definition, completely and utterly awful. But this one seemed worse than most. Or maybe it was just hard to get out of bed because I'd been up late trying to wrestle some words onto the page for my next article. Last I'd checked the board, I was still in second place, behind Joey's comic. And he wasn't letting me forget it—he taunted me every day in journalism. Now I regretted staying up so late. The circles under my eyes were so dark, they'd need a pound of makeup, and I barely had enough energy to drag myself out of bed and to the closet. At least I could wear my pajamas to school in the name of school spirit. One less decision for my tired brain to make. Spirit week started today, which meant homecoming was this Saturday. Of course, I'd messed everything up, so I wasn't feeling particularly spirited.

I'd waited all weekend for Logan to call, but not a word. Not a phone call or text or smoke signal. Each passing hour felt like a nail going into our coffin, and it made me want to shrivel up in the closet or maybe get a cat—or ten—to console myself. Maybe he hadn't made up his mind yet, but honestly, how much time did a guy need?

It was hopeless, but somehow my heart didn't get that memo. All the way to school, it kept coming up with reasons to cut Logan some slack. I couldn't shut it up no matter how many times I told myself it was over.

The hallways were crowded with students barely covering enough skin to stay within the dress code, which was ironic, since my last article had been on the dress code. I saw more than a few guys trying to convince teachers they should be allowed to take off their shirts since they slept that way, and most of the girls were wearing slinky slips that showed more leg than can-can dancers in the Moulin Rouge. By the time lunch came around, probably 20 percent of the student population were wearing their gym clothes because their pajamas had been deemed indecent.

I'd settled on pajama bottoms and a matching tee, but when I got to the cafeteria, I saw that Elena definitely belonged to the Less Is More camp. She was wearing a cute graphic tee and shorts with long, white, knee-high socks (very Ariana Grande of her, Robyn pointed out). I wished I were cool enough to pull off that look.

I watched Elena surreptitiously as Robyn and I went through the lunch line. There weren't any rumors about her and Vince being a couple, though there were plenty about our breakup. Most people didn't know whether to feel sorry for me or blame me, so it was like there was a bubble of silence wherever I went. People would suddenly become quiet when I passed by, and I felt their eyes now as I added a pudding cup to my tray.

The stares didn't bother me as much as I thought they would. It was simply too exhausting to keep up with everyone else's idea of perfect. And in the end, really, what for? Worrying about it in the past hadn't gotten me anything besides one awkward relationship and a whole lot of crazy drama. And I sure didn't need any more of that, thank you very much.

Elena sat with the rest of the student council, half of whom were wearing their gym clothes. Elena was in the center, her shiny hair straight and perfect. She didn't look toward Vince's table, and she didn't actually eat anything. Her fork swirled the spaghetti around her plate, but everything else was untouched.

Robyn and I paid for our lunches and moved to a table close to the doors. Logan was sitting with some of his other friends, but he very pointedly didn't look in my direction. I hesitated for a full five and a half seconds, but I wasn't up for public rejection just yet. I set my tray down with a dejected *thump*.

Still, I couldn't help but watch him. I was pathetic. So, so pathetic. Eventually he looked up, met my eyes, then immediately shifted his gaze away to Robyn. Talk about ouch. The rejection made my cheeks burn.

Then he looked over at Elena, making my blood boil. Did he like Elena? Why had he kissed me then?

I clutched my fork in a death grip and stared down at my plate, practically searing a hole with my gaze.

We'd only been sitting for a few minutes before someone came to our table. I looked up in surprise to see Elena standing across from me, to the left of Robyn. She dropped her tray on the table with a clatter, leaving the Jell-O wiggling. She sat down but didn't say anything. Her look said it all for her. This was one angry bird.

"Ummm . . . hi," I said.

Robyn ate her sandwich silently, her gaze bouncing back and forth between us.

"You know, I'm beginning to question how we were ever friends," Elena said. "How could you do this, Mia?" I stopped breathing while my brain jumped into hyperdrive. Had she found out about the kiss? Did she like Logan now? I was going crazy. I could feel it, but I couldn't help it.

"Okay, I'll bite. What'd I do this time?" I was jittery and angry, so I clamped my hands to my sides to keep them from shaking.

"Seriously?" she asked. "You're going to pretend you don't know what I'm talking about?"

So this *was* about the kiss with Logan. I searched my brain for something to say, but came up empty.

"Like you don't know that Vince came over this weekend to ask me to homecoming?" Elena continued. "When I know for a fact he asked you already. Do you think I'm stupid? You know, after I kissed Logan at mini-golf, I knew you had to have put him up to asking me to homecoming. Because even though he might act like it, he feels nothing for me."

This statement shouldn't have made me so happy, especially because Elena wasn't done chewing me out.

"First Logan, and now Vince. I might suck at school, but I can do the math, Mia. I embarrassed you publicly, and now you're dying for a chance to even the score."

I wanted to argue, but Elena wouldn't even let me get a word in. Everything I wanted to say started to simmer under the surface, biding its time until Elena finally got off her freaking soapbox.

"I'm not falling for it, Mia. So whatever crazy plot you have going on, you can just forget about it. If you were going to have Vince stand me up for homecoming, he won't get the chance. I told him no."

At this, Robyn put the sandwich down. I felt annoyed on Vince's behalf. He wasn't to blame here. He'd actually been downright amazing about everything, and he didn't deserve to have Elena go off on him.

Elena stood up to leave, but I wasn't about to let her have the last word.

"I don't get you," I said, getting up also. "You like Vince, right? So why is it so hard for you to believe he genuinely likes you back? Vince dumped me on Friday, and I thought you'd want to gloat, but no, for some insane reason, you think I've orchestrated a crazy scheme to get back at you. Well, news flash, Elena: I'm over it. I'm over Vince, and I'm over you, and I'm over all of this." I could feel the heat reaching up my neck, but I wouldn't let myself cry, no matter how frustrated I felt in that moment.

"Like I'm supposed to believe that," Elena said, her voice shaking. Her face was getting red, and her hands were clenched into fists. "And you." She pointed at Robyn. "Don't play innocent here. I know your matchmaking business is what caused this mess."

Robyn's eyes got really big. I boiled over. How dare Elena drag Robyn into this?

"Hey now." Robyn stood up also. "I haven't done anything wrong."

"Before you accuse us of anything horrible, Elena, maybe you should look in the mirror." I felt bad as soon as I said it, but it was refreshing at the same time, like eating a lemon.

Elena sucked in a breath and grabbed the yogurt from her tray. I barely had time to read *only 90 calories* on the side of the container before she chucked it at me. It hit the front of my shirt with a splatter, the pink goo dripping down my V-neck.

"Oh no, you didn't," I said, picking up my pudding and tearing off the lid. It was sailing through the air a second later. Elena shrieked and tried to duck behind the bench, but the pudding hit her back with a thump. She squealed like a guinea pig as she twisted around to view the damage.

"This is *designer*," she hissed.

Robyn took a step back, holding her hands in front of her. "You guys—"

"Then it should go with anything. Even chocolate. Oh, and by the way, I'm not sorry." A girl to my right watched us, but other than that, I was surprised by how few people had noticed the catfight going on. Sure, we weren't shouting or anything, but still. How come whenever I wanted to go unnoticed, I couldn't help but become the center of attention, but when I needed someone to see how completely unhinged Elena was acting, no one even cared?

Elena picked up her plastic plate of spaghetti and tapped her finger on the edge.

"Don't," I said, taking a step back. I glanced at Robyn, who looked torn between intervening and going for help.

"Oops," Elena said, drawing back and launching the plate at me. She overestimated, and the plate crashed onto the table behind me, spraying everyone there with spaghetti sauce. It looked like a murder scene from a thriller movie.

Then someone yelled, "Food fight!" and carrots rained down like confetti. Within minutes, all chaos broke loose.

I could imagine the headlines tomorrow. Our features section would have a field day with this, which didn't exactly bode well for my chances in the competition. The cherry on top of what was already a bad day.

I crawled beneath the table but not before getting hit by another cup of yogurt. Strawberry, of course. My shirt would probably have a pink blotch for all eternity. It all started piling up on the floor around me, a literal minefield of questionable school lunch food. A second later, Robyn joined me.

"Well, this is fun," she said, picking something red off her pants.

Through the opening between the benches and the table, I could see students scurrying to get out of the way of flying spaghetti. A carton of milk landed a foot away from where we crouched, sloshing liquid all over and spraying my face.

The noise in the cafeteria reached roar status, and I could no longer distinguish one shriek from another. A foot stepped into the spilled milk and someone came crashing down next to me, landing on the tile floor with a whoosh.

"Oh my— Logan, are you all right?" I asked, helping him crawl beneath the table for shelter. He rubbed the back of his head and grinned.

"You know, I shouldn't be surprised you're in the middle of all this," he said. "Do you go looking for drama, or does it just seem to find you?" I wanted to kiss the smirk off his lips, but one quip wasn't enough to convince me all was right between us. He'd gone all weekend without calling me, after all. I tried to stay mad, but this close proximity was doing funny things to my brain. With all the noise and motion around me, I was already dizzy enough. I sat back and put as much distance between us as I could, which wasn't a whole lot. We were camping out underneath a lunch table, after all, and Robyn wouldn't move over.

Logan shifted his weight so he could see more of what was happening. He cradled his camera protectively with one hand, even though it was still in its case. He kept fiddling with the strap like he was itching to take pictures of all the action but didn't want to risk damaging his baby.

A packet of ketchup flew past his nose, and he dropped his hand. "You looked pretty mad. Are *you* okay?" He turned to me then, and I tried to read the expression on his face. A flurry of hope made my heart beat faster, but it was squashed just as quickly when he added, "Where is Elena, anyway?"

"I don't know, and I don't care," I said. One side of his lips quirked up in his token half smile, deflating my anger somewhat. A stampede of feet ran past our table, and one student slammed into it. I jerked back and fell against Logan, who steadied me with his hands. When he didn't remove them, I almost stopped breathing.

"What were you arguing about?" he asked. I could barely hear him over all the noise, his voice just above a whisper. Robyn was focused on the world outside our little bubble, and I felt myself relax against Logan.

"Stupid stuff. Vince asked her to homecoming. She thinks he's only pretending to like her."

Logan's eyebrows drew together, and his gaze darted to Robyn, who was wiping her hands on her jeans.

"Vince really likes Elena," I said. Then, because I remembered our conversation from the tree house, I added, "And I am completely fine with that." A crash sounded nearby, but I didn't turn. I needed to see Logan's reaction.

Logan's face was unreadable. He was so good at hiding his emotions that it made me want to scream. Not that my screaming would have been heard over all the commotion going on around us. The food seemed to be flying at a slower pace now, probably because most of it had already been thrown.

The atmosphere in the lunchroom suddenly shifted, and I heard whispers of "The principal's coming!" spreading through the crowd.

"Not. Good." Robyn started to get out. And she probably had the right idea. If Principal Egeus found out I'd been instrumental in starting the food fight, my perfect school record would be shot. Logan helped me crawl out from under the table, and I scanned the floor for the best exit route. I was too late, though.

The principal walked into the cafeteria, and there wasn't a student there who wasn't intimidated. *Everything* about him demanded respect. He was six feet four inches of solid muscle and probably could have passed as a tank if he stood still for long enough in the school parking lot.

He surveyed the cafeteria silently. He took in the spaghetti sauce on the walls, the smashed fruit on the floors, the broken trophy display case— I did a double take. When had *that* happened? Shattered glass littered the floor surrounding it, and jagged edges framed the gaping hole in front.

I looked back at Principal Egeus to see his reaction, and his face was all hard lines. This wasn't going to be pretty.

"You've all demonstrated a deplorable lack of respect for your school and faculty." His deep voice echoed off the walls. "Not to mention you risked the safety of your fellow students.

Everyone here will face consequences for what happened today."

Part of me wondered how he planned on punishing over one hundred students at once. It wasn't like we'd all fit in detention.

"Who started this?" Principal Egeus asked, and my pulse beat double time. My face felt hot, like a flare lighting up my guilt, but no one said anything. Maybe it had all started so fast that no one really knew the cause. But no, that wasn't true. Logan had been watching. He knew. But he didn't say anything either.

The principal pursed his lips. "Fine. You will all leave the cafeteria in a single-file line. On your way out, you will give your name to my secretary, and lest anyone feel like making up a name, know that she'll be checking names against your school photos from your accounts." He handed his tablet to his secretary, who I hadn't even noticed was standing behind him. I was guessing he already had the directory up and running.

"Each of you will be required to perform ten hours of community service. I expect a letter of completion, signed and certified from whatever organization you choose to inflict with your sorry presence. We will post a sign-up with suitable organizations on the office's door by the end of school today. You have three weeks to find the time."

With that, he walked away without a single crack in his demeanor. I let out a breath and thanked my lucky stars that Logan liked Elena enough not to rat us out. Maybe it was for me—at least, I wanted to think that, but even with everything else that had happened, the most depressing thought of the day was this: In all probability, Logan was still hung up on Elena. And that thought sucked a whole lot more than a thousand yogurt-stained shirts.

twenty-one

There were so many students crowding around the sign-ups after school on Monday that I didn't get a good look at the list until Tuesday morning. There were the usual places—the public library, the humane society, and a lot of other organizations that I'd seen on television commercials. Robyn would love the one with puppies, so I signed her up. She had some article she was working on, and she'd asked me to pick one for her. Last I checked in, she'd been busily tapping away at her computer, too busy to even glance up.

My finger trailed down the list, searching for one that might somehow look good on my college applications. There was nothing for a budding reporter. My finger stopped on something else, though. Logan's name. He'd signed up to mentor elementary kids in some kind of reading program I'd never heard of before. There were two empty slots beneath his name, and I hastily claimed one. With three weeks to finish our community service and only ten hours to complete, the odds weren't good that I'd ever see him there. Still, I was going to take every chance I could get.

I turned around and came face-to-face with Elena. Because of spirit week, most people were wearing togas made out of bedsheets today. Elena's outfit was classier, though, the silky pleats a definite step up from bedsheets and tablecloths.

Maybe in the past, we would have laughed about how she'd organized spirit week so she could wear this dress she'd found earlier, or maybe she would have joked about how much of a prude I was for never showing my legs. But those days felt blurry in my memory.

"Excuse me," she said. It was funny how those words could sound so impolite coming from her lips.

I moved to the side so she could see the sign-up list. My heart was hammering in my ribs, and I wasn't really sure why I stuck around. Old habits died hard, though. I searched for the right words to say, but my brain was completely blanking. *Sorry?* That wasn't exactly true. *Let's pretend none of this ever happened?* Fat chance. *Can we just move on already?* That was a lukewarm attempt at best. How could I come up with words when I didn't even know what I wanted? Still, part of me ached at what we'd become.

"Nice school spirit," I said, motioning toward her dress. I think I meant it as a compliment, but I wasn't really sure.

"Nice lack of it," she said, taking in my non-Greek outfit.

"I wore my gold bangles," I said, holding up my arm for inspection. "That's about as Greek as I get."

"Whatever." Elena cocked her hip while she studied the list. A few seconds later, my Logan radar went off. He rounded the corner, talking to Vince of all people. Not that they looked chummy or anything. Pretty much the opposite.

Elena saw them and sighed in response. I heard her mumble something about wishing they'd just leave her alone already, and I felt a momentary surge of satisfaction. Vindication burned through my veins, and I held back a smile. It served her right. Of course, as soon as I thought that, I hated myself for it. What kind of friend was I, wishing that on people?

Logan and Vince spotted us. Robyn thought Logan would come around in time, but I was beginning to have my doubts. In that moment, I couldn't tell whether he was looking at me or Elena. And since we still hadn't really talked about the kiss, I was beginning to feel like maybe I'd imagined it.

"Hey there," Vince said when they reached us.

Elena tossed her hair over her shoulder and crossed her arms. "Are you trying to flirt with me or her? These days it's hard to tell."

Vince let out a breath. "Come on, Elena," he said. He reached out, then seemingly thought twice and lowered his arm. "You know I never really liked Mia." Of course, I knew Vince's past feelings for me weren't real. He'd only asked me out from obligation. But still. Talk about ouch. I *had* liked him.

I noticed Logan was watching me and my reaction to the conversation. Did he still think I was hung up on Vince? Was that why he was giving me time? Time was the last thing I wanted right now. Time sucked. Time could drive off a cliff.

Then a weight seemed to hit my chest. Maybe he wasn't giving me time. Maybe he was giving me the cold shoulder because he liked Elena.

"Come on, man, she's right there. You could at least try to be nice," Logan said, and the weight on my chest lessened just a bit, even though I was keeping my expectations low. Defending me didn't mean he liked me. I needed to get that through my thick skull. But it was no use. I still smiled. Sheesh, I was pathetic. It wasn't even like Logan had said something super nice or anything. For all I knew, he could be thinking the same thing as Vince, but he could be better at hiding it.

Elena was watching Vince closely. She gave a huff and abruptly turned back to the community-service sheet, leaving me wondering what she'd been thinking. Maybe she was finally coming around and would stop giving Vince a hard time.

And maybe pigs would fly.

She tapped a finger on her hip.

"You know, last I checked, there was still a spot open with me," Logan said.

"Like Elena would want to spend more time with you than absolutely necessary," Vince said.

Wait. Had Logan been hinting for *Elena* to join him for

community service? Or me? Maybe I'd read him wrong. After all, Logan did seem to bristle at Vince's comment. But then again, he could have been upset simply because Vince was being rude.

My brain hurt from trying to sort everything out. Was it asking too much simply to want concrete answers? *Come on, universe, throw me a bone already.*

Vince laughed. "What am I saying? Never mind. It's not like you're competition." I clenched my hands at my side.

"Really?" Logan stepped closer to Vince. They were only a foot apart. "If I'm not competition, then explain why Mia here had such a hard time deciding between us? And why I'm the one who came out on top?"

Oh good, now I was being dragged into the discussion. Well, there were pros and cons to this. I mean, on one hand, Logan had mentioned me, which meant I was still on his mind. Kind of. But on the other, he only mentioned me in an argument over whether Elena considered him Vince's competition, so that probably didn't count. It certainly seemed like he wasn't over Elena yet. Ugh. This conversation was the worst, and there was nothing I could do about it besides stand here with a frozen smile.

Elena's smug look wasn't helping things, either. I took a step back, trying to decide whether anyone would notice if I walked away. Anywhere else would have been preferable. Siberia. Calculus class. I'd take it if it meant I didn't have to stand here and watch the guy I liked argue over another girl.

Vince stiffened but didn't say anything to Logan's comment. Instead he picked up the pen that was hanging next to the sign-up sheet and wrote Elena's name deliberately next to his own, helping out at the recycling center. He stepped back and raised an eyebrow to Logan.

"Nice of you to decide for her," Logan said. "As if you'd ever know what a girl wanted, even if it hit you in the face."

Vince clenched his jaw and took another step toward Logan. "Oh yeah?" he said. "You mean like this?"

And then Vince punched Logan in the face.

It all happened so quickly. One minute we were standing there calmly, albeit a little tense, and the next, Vince and Logan were fighting in the hallway. My hand flew up to my mouth and a squeak escaped. Elena's eyes were wide, but she couldn't look away from the two boys duking it out in front of us.

Like me, Elena seemed incapable of movement. She didn't even step back but instead stayed cemented to the spot in front of the sign-ups. Logan tucked his shoulder and barreled into Vince, tackling him to the ground. For a star athlete, Vince went down surprisingly easy. He was only down for a second, though, and he sprang up just as quickly.

I'd never actually seen a fight in real life. It wasn't so much a fistfight as it was a mixture of wrestling and grabbing. Vince jumped up and pulled-slash-shoved Logan, who crashed into a large plastic trash bin. Garbage flew everywhere, and the gray bin spun on its side. I sidestepped someone's discarded banana and hesitated, torn between going for help and staying as a witness. At most, the fight had been going on for a few seconds, but it felt like time had slowed down. Their arms locked around each other's heads, and they hit the wall with their shoulders. Neither of them were shouting, like I'd expected, but I could easily hear each crash and curse in the otherwise silent hallway.

They were getting a little too close for comfort, so I backed up, into the office door. I was so jittery that my elbows knocked loudly on the wood, and that was when I knew we were all in for trouble.

The door opened behind me, and I stumbled backward. I found myself staring at Principal Egeus, who looked angry enough to kill. And I wouldn't have put it past him.

In two steps, he reached Logan and Vince and pulled them apart. Logan rubbed his jaw, and Vince rolled his shoulders like he was working out a sore spot.

"My office. Now," Principal Egeus barked, and released them, stumbling, in my direction. I scooted to the side of the doorway, allowing them to pass. Looking around, I wondered if I was supposed to be included in that order. The principal answered my question by pointing a finger first at Elena and then at me and then at his office. We got the hint.

Logan stood in one corner while Vince leaned against the opposite wall. The tension between them wasn't dimmed by the distance, though. Their eyes were locked on each other, some kind of silent standoff happening in their gaze. If someone had walked into their line of sight, they'd probably be incinerated on the spot. Elena and I took the two chairs facing the principal's desk, even though that felt like the worst possible place to be in that moment.

Principal Egeus came in then, and the door slammed shut behind him. He walked to his desk and sat down, fixing us each with a solid glare.

"Well?" he asked. "Who's first?"

We all exchanged awkward looks while waiting for someone to break the silence. It wasn't like I was going to volunteer anything. The less the principal knew about my involvement, the better. Logan finally cleared his throat and said, "We're sorry things got out of hand, sir."

The principal turned his attention to him, putting the brunt of his angry stare on Logan.

"But Vince started it," I said, surprising myself.

"Did I ask who started it?" the principal asked, and I swallowed. "I don't care who started it. I want to know why it escalated to the point of spilling blood on school soil." Yeah, he said *school soil* as if this were some kind of hallowed ground. But then my brain caught up to what he'd said, and the word *blood* caused me to shift in my seat so I could see Logan better. He was lightly gripping his arm, where I could see a long scratch between his fingers. Principal Egeus yanked a few tissues from a box and held them out to Logan. "Don't bleed on my carpet."

Logan took the tissues and retreated back to his corner. The principal turned to Elena.

"Since you weren't involved physically, maybe you can tell me honestly what happened," he said, proving how little he knew us. Didn't he know she wrote the gossip column? "You may begin."

Elena hesitated, looking at each of us in turn. When her eyes connected with mine, I could almost feel her apology, and it made me pause. In a soft monotone voice, Elena began recounting the last few minutes in the hall. She didn't paint me as a villain, and I wasn't sure what to think about that. Everything about her posture suggested defeat, and surprisingly, I sympathized. I sat and listened to her talk, feeling bad about everything.

The whole story didn't take long to tell.

"Then Mia backed into the door. That's when you got there," she finished. We sat quietly, awaiting the principal's verdict.

"You're saying this is all a lover's spat," he said. "Am I understanding things correctly?"

No one answered. We didn't need to. Elena half-smiled uncomfortably under the principal's stare. He picked up a pen and tapped it on the edge of his desk while he considered us. The taps got louder and louder as we waited for his decision.

"You are all suspended for the rest of the week," he said, folding his arms across his chest.

Suspended. The word echoed in my head, refusing to make sense. Suspended. Me, the good student. The one with career goals and the drive to make them happen.

What was worse, I actually felt I deserved it.

My eyes started to sting, and I desperately tried to calm

down so that no one, especially Elena, could see how much this news affected me. I could picture the headline of her next article now, and it was worse than the first. Sure, she seemed contrite, but I wasn't sure if I could trust that any more than I could trust Robyn's younger twin brothers not to raid my underwear drawer.

"During the suspension, you will not be allowed on school grounds and you will not be permitted at school activities, including homecoming," the principal continued. "The soccer team will be playing without you, Vince, and Elena, your name will be removed from the homecoming court." At least he hadn't said I was disqualified from the journalism competition. Maybe he didn't really know about it. I wasn't about to remind him.

"But Elena and Mia weren't involved," Logan interjected. "This was between me and Vince."

"They weren't involved somehow?" Principal Egeus said. "You don't think they deserve the suspension? Then why have several sources come to me with the information that they started the food fight yesterday? I don't know all that is going on between you four, but let me assure you, it has no place at Athens High."

We were all silent.

"My secretary will prepare some papers for you to take home to your families. Your parents are welcome to call me to discuss the terms of your suspension, which is effective immediately." There was that word again, echoing around because my brain was too slow to process what was happening. *Suspension*. My head actually hurt from thinking about it. The back of my throat burned. I tried to stop my hands from shaking by placing them in my lap. How had it come to this? This was something that would be on my record forever. It would affect what colleges I got into. Colleges would determine my future jobs. My whole career as a journalist might go up in flames. Getting suspended would change everything I'd planned for my life. I had to sniff a few times so my nose wouldn't drip. This was worse than anything I could imagine.

"Now"—he looked at each of us in turn—"you can call your parents and tell them the news."

twenty-two

I moped for the rest of the day. Well, moped and did homework. Only, I did it at my dad's office, because he "couldn't trust me alone anymore." I tried pointing out that I hadn't been alone when the whole suspension thing went down, but then he frowned and gave me *the look*. The one that made me want to hunker down in a bomb shelter for the next fifty years until the storm passed. That look.

My mom had already called the principal three times, going off on the injustice of it all. But my dad? No, my dad decided now was the perfect time to play a drill sergeant. As if I needed someone else making me feel bad about everything. Like I wasn't doing a good enough job of that myself. I threw myself into my homework, hoping it would distract me from my dark, spiraling thoughts, but even that didn't work. No matter what I did, I was still completely and utterly defeated.

My parents might have been on opposite sides of the fence in this matter, but they agreed on one thing: My phone privileges were taken away for a whole month. Joke was on them. I didn't have anyone to talk to. Even Robyn had been acting weird and flaky lately, and I'd alienated everyone else.

My dad had a pretty large office, but it was much safer to do my homework in an empty cubicle. Occasionally he'd stick his head out and make sure I was still alive, and whenever he did this, I wondered if he was disappointed that I was. That was how crestfallen he looked, and it only made me feel worse.

"How's that calculus coming along?" he asked on his way back from the break room.

"Fine," I answered, keeping my eyes on the book.

"Will you come into my office for a minute?" he said. That sick feeling in my stomach returned, and I hurriedly shoved everything back in my bag and followed after him. He closed the door after me, and I tried to disappear into one of his leather armchairs. My dad was the vice president of a small, laid-back advertising company, and they were all about appearances. While the chairs looked nice, they weren't exactly comfortable. Then again, nothing about this situation was comfortable.

He sighed as he sat down.

"You're a good kid, you know that?" he asked. I shifted in my chair. "Listen, I know we've come down hard on you, and the truth is, this is the first time you've ever given us serious grief, so I suppose I should be happy about that." He gave a wan smile. "Are you doing okay? This can't be easy on you."

"I deserve it," I said.

He nodded and placed his hands on his desk. "You think you'll be ready to leave in a few minutes? How are you coming on your homework?"

"Dad, I've been at your office all day with nothing to do but homework. I'm *ahead* on it all. I only have one journalism article left." I couldn't bring myself to work on that. I knew I was only delaying the inevitable, but there was so much pressure to come up with something mind-blowingly amazing for the competition. After all, I'd just destroyed my chances of getting into a good school. This competition was my last chance. But I didn't think I was capable of writing the kind of article I'd need.

"All right, I won't force you to come with me to work tomorrow." Dad smiled. "Think you can call that elementary school about completing some of your community service hours?"

"Does that mean I get my phone back?" I asked.

"Don't push your luck," he said. "You can use the home phone." He stood up. "All right, give me a few minutes to wrap things up. Our head copywriter quit, and I have one more interview before we go home."

"You need to hire one before you can finish your site redesign, don't you?" I asked, an idea taking root in my mind.

"Unfortunately," he said, leafing through a few papers he held.

"I could do it."

My dad's eyes snapped up, meeting mine over the top of

the papers. "You can't be our head copywriter. The position is full-time."

"No." I stood up. "I want to write your website copy." This was my answer. The way I was going to pay Robyn back for the money I'd lost her. Finally there was something I could do besides feel sorry for myself. I just *needed* my dad to agree. "Think about it. I know your advertising company better than any new copywriter could. I know who you've worked with before, and I know what you've done for them. While your new copywriter is learning the ropes, I can finish the website copy, and that way your site redesign won't be delayed. You can pay me what you pay your freelancers." I waited, being sure to keep my hands still by my sides, even though they itched to fiddle with something. "That way you can take your time finding the right copywriter instead of hurrying because of your site."

My dad gave me a considering look.

"You're ahead on all your homework?" he asked. I nodded, and he tapped his finger on the edge of the stack of papers. "Let me talk to HR."

He smiled as he left.

This time I stayed in his office. There seemed to be a few warm fuzzies in here, and I could sure use more of those in my life.

I didn't have any problem setting up my community service hours. The elementary school said most of the high school students wanted to help with the after-school program, so they could use the help during the regular school day. I showed up at eight thirty Wednesday morning, ready for a full day of what basically amounted to glorified babysitting.

Athens Elementary had a separate room where they tutored children who struggled with reading, and they lumped all the students together regardless of age. It was like a study hall where kids came and went whenever their teachers were doing a reading unit.

When I arrived, four other people were in the room. An elementary-school teacher, two students . . . and Logan. He looked up when I entered, but I could barely meet his eyes. Too much had happened. Simply seeing him made me feel like I'd gotten off on the wrong exit and was trying to navigate without any phone or map.

He'd actually thrown punches at Vince, and I could only see him doing that if he was interested in Elena, which made his stance pretty freaking clear. It sucked, but it was time I took a hint. We'd kissed. He'd ignored me. For *days*. He'd gotten into a fight over someone else. Try as I might to change his mind, a girl could only take so much rejection.

Admitting that felt worse than getting suspended, which was something I never thought was possible. I had a raw, gaping hole in my chest, and I'd already tried filling it with chocolate. Robyn was right—being someone's second choice was worse than never making it into the running.

I dropped my bag on the nearest desk in defeat. As far as

I could tell, there really was nothing to be done. Logan walked over to where I was, and I plastered on my *I'm okay* face.

"Looks like we had the same idea—to get the community service out of the way," he said. I gave him a feeble smile.

The teacher walked over to us. "You must be Mia," she said, holding out her hand. "I'm so glad you and Logan could come in today. That means I'll be able to help out with the math tutoring down the hall." I must have looked worried, because she smiled reassuringly. "Don't worry, you'll be fine. Students bring a paper with them. It says everything they need to work on, and each tutoring session only lasts thirty minutes. It can sometimes get pretty empty, so you might have a lot of downtime. If you need me, my name is Mrs. Stephens, and I'll be in room 121." It wasn't the tutoring I was worried about but rather being alone with Logan. Too bad Mrs. Stephens didn't take that into account.

She left, and I couldn't think of a single thing to say to Logan. Instead I squatted down in front of one of the students and asked her what she was working on. Logan went to help the other student.

The little girl in front of me studied me quizzically. She was maybe in the first grade, but I wasn't exactly a kid person, so I was probably a poor judge.

"What are you hiding from?" she asked.

"Hiding? I'm not hiding," I said.

"Then why are you crouched by the desk?"

I sat in the desk next to her and scooted it close so I could see her paper. She held it out like it was contagious.

"My teacher says I need to practice my *sight words*." It was obvious that she put *sight words* in the same category as things like tetanus shots and cooties.

"Well," I said, flipping open her practice book. I looked at the name scrawled across the top in child-formed letters. "Chloe, let's start with—"

"What's his name? He's cute," she said, pointing to Logan.

So much for cooties.

"His name is Logan," I said, trying to sound nonchalant. Logan looked up at the sound of his name, and I put all my focus into avoiding his gaze.

"Are you two married?" she asked.

"No!" I said a bit too quickly. Logan smirked, and I felt my cheeks burn. "We're only in high school."

"So is he your boyfriend?" she asked. Would this girl never stop?

"No."

"Oh," she said, looking at me with pity in her eyes. "Do you *have* a boyfriend?"

I took a deep breath.

"No."

"Well, *I* have a boyfriend," she said, and I ground my teeth. From his corner, I could hear Logan stifle a chuckle. "His name is Jason, and he pushes me on the swings."

"That's . . . nice."

"I can help you get a boyfriend," she said. "All you do is scream and run away when they chase you."

Now Logan was really laughing. "That's about right," he said in between fits. I sent him a glare, but that only encouraged him. From the glint in his eyes, I could tell he was enjoying this immensely.

When thirty minutes were up, it was a relief. Even if that meant I was now alone with Logan. *Alone* alone, this time. No students came in after Chloe and the other student left, so it was just him and me filling up the small room with our silence.

He leaned back in his desk and turned his upper body to face me.

"So," he said. "Are we back to square one?"

"What do you mean?" I asked.

"When you wanted nothing to do with me and wouldn't talk to me even if we were the only two people in a room."

My cheeks flushed. "What? No, of course not," I said. "I'm talking to you now, aren't I?"

He raised his eyebrows. "Your conversation skills are a little rusty."

"Well, what do you want me to say?" I asked. "I mean, you got into a fight over Elena right after I confessed my feelings for you. Right after we kissed. There isn't much more for me to talk about."

Logan grinned. "You're cute when you're jealous, you know," he said. He leaned forward and rested his elbows on the desk. I couldn't help but notice the way it stretched his shirt across his broad shoulders. The room was so quiet, I felt for sure he could hear my heart beating.

I waited before saying anything to make sure I could trust my voice. "Who says I'm jealous?"

Logan raised his eyebrows, and I knew I'd been caught in my lie.

"Fine. Not that it matters to you," I said, leaning back and crossing my arms.

"Mia." He stood up and walked over to where I was sitting, choosing a chair across from me. He took my hand in his, and I worried he'd be able to feel my rapidly beating pulse there. "I'm too old to chase you on the playground, so I'm doing my best with what I've got."

"If you're saying you like me, you've got a strange way of showing it."

He took a deep breath and let it out. "I never stopped liking you."

The jagged edges around my heart softened a little.

"But you asked Elena to homecoming," I said, relishing the feel of my hand in his. Logan smiled, and I started breathing again. It was the first glimmer of hope I'd felt since I'd ruined everything.

"I asked Elena because Robyn told me to. She thought it'd make you jealous. And it seemed to be working, so I went with it." He shrugged. "But I wasn't supposed to kiss you. Robyn wanted me to play hard to get. I worried I'd ruined everything for us and that article she was working on."

This made me pause.

"What?"

"Come on, Mia. You know how stubborn you are. I think you just needed some time to sort it all out."

That wasn't what I was asking. He'd said something about an article, and I wanted to know more.

"Then I was worried you still liked Vince, and I didn't want to push you. What if you were rebounding? Then I didn't want to get on Vince's bad side, and, well, we all know how that turned out. But I'm so sick of letting Robyn, or Vince, control me. They can just deal. I need to be honest."

"Honesty is usually the best policy, or so I've heard." Especially if it led to confessions like this. I could get used to these. For the first time in a long time, I felt full to the brim with happiness.

"I'm a fan."

"Of honesty? Or me?" I waggled my eyebrows.

Logan smiled. "Both," he said, stroking my hand. I was gooey all over, like fresh chocolate-chip cookies.

"I think the only way relationships work is if people are one hundred percent honest with each other. No secrets."

"One hundred percent?" I asked, the familiar feeling of guilt starting to creep into my stomach. There were so many things I hadn't told Logan, and some of them might make him hate me. Like how I'd emailed Vince my name and set this whole thing in motion. "Not even little white lies?" I let go of his hand, and he hesitated.

"Maybe the good kinds of lies. The ones people laugh about when they all work out. Like surprise gifts."

Mine so weren't that kind. I took a breath and debated

my options. I should tell him. I didn't need this blowing up in my face later. Knowing my luck, it probably would no matter what.

"Logan." I swallowed, placing my hands on my knees. It was now or never. "All of this was my fault. The suspension, everything."

"How could this possibly be your fault?" he asked.

The words lumped in my throat. I took his hand again, needing the warmth of it to give me courage. The feeling of his skin against mine gave me second (and third, and fourth) thoughts, but I plunged ahead before he could do anything like kiss me.

"Because I went behind Robyn's back and matched Vince with me. I sent him the email that started all this." I explained everything then, leaving nothing out. He looked cautious, which was only to be expected, but he listened to my whole explanation without interrupting. I confessed what I'd really been doing when he'd caught me breaking into the computer lab that day. I told him how none of this would have happened if only I'd listened to Robyn in the first place.

Logan drew in a breath. He didn't speak for a moment, and I could count each of my heartbeats in the silence.

"Well," he said. "That sucks." He ran a hand through his hair. "But I guess I already knew you liked him. So even if I hate it, it's not exactly a news flash."

He didn't sound forgiving. It was more like he was trying to convince himself. I felt the despair creeping back in, and I desperately tried to keep it at bay. Now was not the time to panic. My heart was fluttering in my rib cage, and I told my pulse to take a chill pill already. It wasn't like he was rejecting me outright.

He squeezed my hand.

"I know you didn't want to make things hard for Robyn's matchmaking gig. I get it. And you came around eventually. I just had to work a little harder to win you over."

All wasn't forgiven, I could tell by the way he took slow breaths and nodded to himself. I remembered what he'd said about bad news, which made my own breathing come faster. How stupid did I have to be, to basically hand-deliver bad news without any sugarcoating? "Just give me a little time to process everything, okay? This wasn't what I was expecting."

I nodded quickly. All in all, things could have gone a lot worse. I tried to remind my racing heart of that. I hated not knowing where that left us officially, but I could deal. I had to.

More students came in then, and we separated to work with them. I was helping a fifth-grade boy with his spelling when I ran out of room on his worksheet.

"Hang on, I just need more paper," I told him, standing up.

Logan was sitting by my backpack.

"I can grab it for you," he said. As if it was so difficult for me to walk the twenty steps over. But I could tell he was trying to be nice, because of everything that had just happened, so I gave in.

"Thanks. It's just in my notebook." I knelt back down and looked over the spelling list again while Logan rummaged in my bag.

A minute later Logan placed a blank sheet of paper on the desk in front of me, his hand shaking. I looked up and watched as he simply walked out of the room.

"Logan?" I called. He didn't answer. I stood up and walked to the door, but Logan was already halfway down the hallway to the main entrance. I hesitated there. It wasn't like I could leave the kids here alone. Maybe Logan just needed to use the bathroom.

I finished the tutoring session, but Logan never came back. When I retrieved my notebook and backpack, I understood why.

Lying on top of my notebook was a paper Logan must have found while getting me the scratch paper I'd asked for.

It was my old pros-and-cons list. The same list where I'd painstakingly written down each and every horrible, awful thing I'd ever thought about Logan. That list.

twenty-three

Sweats? Check. Unwashed hair pulled into a bun? Check. Puffy eyes? Definitely a check. Ice cream? Well, that one was nonexistent, since I'd eaten every last bit we owned, including the freezer-burned vanilla that no one had touched since last Thanksgiving. And the other stuff was dairy-free and low calorie, so it wouldn't fill the gaping hole in my heart.

I wasn't in school and I'd finished my dad's website copy, so I should have been happy. But right now, I couldn't even remember what happy felt like. It was like a dark fog had sucked all that away, leaving me with nothing but a sharp emptiness. Each moment with Logan felt glassy, removed and out of reach. All I could remember was this moment now, lying on the couch in front of the television, clutching the stuffed unicorn I'd gotten at the Pier with Logan. I was weighed down with the knowledge, absolute and certain, that we could never come back from this. And because I didn't have my phone and my parents had kicked me off the internet, there was no way I could explain why I'd written that stupid pros-and-cons list forever ago.

Funnily enough, I actually missed Elena more now than I had in the past several days. She would have made me laugh. She would have done something crazy to take my mind off my imploding relationship. But she was gone, too.

There weren't many shows to choose from on Wednesday afternoons, so I was left with an overly dramatic sitcom that I didn't bother trying to follow. I'd already watched everything in my Netflix queue. My mom had dropped me off hours ago from volunteering, but I hadn't moved recently, except to go to the bathroom when my bladder couldn't take it anymore. I didn't want to move from this couch ever again. Moving took motivation, and I had none.

I tried to push myself farther into the couch, begging it to swallow me whole. The fabric was soft against my cheek, but I didn't feel like I deserved even that small mercy. The roughest, scratchiest fabric in the world wouldn't have been enough to reflect how I felt inside. It wasn't just that Logan wanted nothing to do with me, it was what I'd done to him. *I* had done this. I couldn't justify it or blame it on someone else. It was all me. Coming face-to-face with this fact was a painful reality to swallow.

When my mom came home a little while later, it was to find me sobbing at the TV, yelling that Kirsten should have forgiven Hayden because it wasn't his fault his boss had fired him for being attractive. At least, that's what I thought had happened. It was a little hard to tell, since I hadn't watched any previous episodes and I kept crying too much to hear the dialogue.

"Okay," my mom said as she stood in front of the television. "I was willing to give you some slack when I dropped you off, but this has to stop. Tell me what happened."

She put her hands on her hips, so I was supposed to take her seriously, but all I could do was bury my head and cry into a couch cushion, which still hadn't dried from the last time I'd done that.

She threw her hands up in frustration and walked into the kitchen.

"You know you're supposed to be at Elena's in an hour?" she called out over her shoulder.

"What? Why?" Elena's was the last place on earth I wanted to be. I'd already tortured myself today. I didn't need my former friend to jump on that train, too. Even if I did miss her, I wanted the *old* her.

"She called this morning while you were in the shower. She said she'd like to talk, and I thought that's what you wanted."

My head was pounding. Couldn't my mom see that this was so not the time to have a little makeup meeting with Elena?

I turned away, my eyes burning. I vaguely heard my mom doing something in the kitchen, ignoring me. The microwave beeped. She came back a few seconds later with a cup of tea in her hands. She held it out to me, and I took it, mostly so she would leave me alone. But she didn't. She sat down beside me and pulled one leg up onto the couch.

"Seems to me like you need your friends now more than ever. What's this all about?" she asked. "A boy, I'm guessing."

I nodded glumly, not trusting the words to come out right.

"Vince?" she asked, and I had to give her points for remembering his name.

"No," I said into my cup of tea.

She huffed as she relaxed into the couch. "I don't know why I bother trying to keep up," she muttered. I heard the garage door open. When my dad opened the door and saw us sitting on the couch, his caterpillar eyebrows practically crawled into his hairline.

"I'll, uh, go get dinner ready," he said, unprepared for coping with teenage hormones.

"I'll help," my mom said, standing up and giving me a look, finally leaving me in peace.

They banged pots to cover up their hushed conversation, but I could hear them whispering. I turned my attention back to the TV and cried again when I saw that Hayden was at the airport, alone with just his bags. If I kept this up, I'd use up all my tears before going to Elena's house later, which, come to think of it, wasn't a bad plan.

Eating dinner with my family was a quiet affair. I'd finally stopped crying, but that didn't stop my parents from exchanging loaded looks over their spaghetti. Food was the last thing on my mind, but I swallowed a few bites to appease them.

"Mia, you should probably get going soon," my dad said, setting his fork on his plate. "Weren't you going to Elena's? Do you need to get ready?"

My scowl must have been effective, because he raised his hands in surrender and pushed his chair away from the table. Mom intervened. "Fine, it's your decision."

It wasn't much of one. I walked over to Elena's, kicking a few rocks out of my path while wondering if I'd made the right choice or if I was just a glutton for punishment. I knocked on the door, then hung back in the shadows, hoping to be overlooked. Maybe no one was home.

No such luck. Elena's dad opened the door, then called for her when he saw me.

"Hey, Mia." She came to his side, then shuffled back somewhat awkwardly, allowing me to enter. We went into their sitting room, and I perched uncomfortably at the edge of the couch, with Elena sitting on the piano bench across from me. Her dad left, thankfully, probably going off to eavesdrop from the stairway landing just around the corner.

"I'm glad you were able to come tonight," Elena said, shifting on the bench. "Can I start?"

I shrugged in what could have passed for acceptance and prepared for another tirade. I was pretty sure I looked like something a cat had thrown up, but Elena was perfectly polished and put together. I never understood how she did that. Like, how did she make her eyes look so large and innocent? Makeup sorcery, that's what it was.

"Mia," Elena said, somewhat shakily, "I owe you an

apology." She gave a faint smile, and it actually looked genuine. Shocker. Maybe all that acting practice was paying off. "I kept blaming you, and I'm sorry about that. I've had a lot of time to think about things, and I know now that everything we fought about was really my fault."

I almost laughed. Maybe she was feeling warm and fuzzy, but I certainly wasn't. Especially considering I'd spent the last several hours curled up in the fetal position and Elena wasn't exactly blameless here. She'd been sending a lot of frost my way lately. Did she seriously think I'd forgive everything she'd done simply because she apologized? Fat chance.

"Vince and I had a long talk yesterday morning," she said. This time when she smiled, I *knew* it was genuine. "We're together now."

I wanted to say *Good for you*, but I held it back. I wasn't feeling exactly charitable, though, and it must have shown in my expression, because she flushed.

"Right, sorry," she said, giving her head a shake. "That's not what's important. What I mean is, I'm sorry I thought you put Vince up to everything, like making him act like he liked me and all that. I don't believe that anymore, obviously."

Against my will, I felt myself softening.

"I'm glad you guys worked it all out," I said. "At least that makes one of us."

Her face scrunched up a little at that.

"That's something I still don't understand." She looked toward the stairs and then, seeing her dad nowhere in sight, continued at a slightly lower volume. "Vince told me about the email. But why'd you email him through Robyn's Cupid thingy if you're so obviously supposed to be with Logan? I mean, everyone can tell how much you guys are into each other."

I wasn't sure whether to laugh or cry. My eyes stung, and I blinked before tears could spill over. Simply hearing Logan's name brought everything back, and I wondered how long I'd be carrying this burning ache in my chest.

But did I really want to confide in Elena? She'd apologized, but that didn't mean the slate was wiped clean. Then again, if I didn't start behaving like her friend, maybe we'd never get back to where we once were.

"I was in denial, I guess." Maybe I wasn't building bridges yet, but at least I wasn't burning them down. "I'm sorry about throwing pudding at you," I said, changing the subject. "Did your shirt stain?"

She waved her hand and her forehead creased. "It was from last season, anyway. I really am sorry, Mia. I wanted to tell you that I've been a complete b—" She paused and very consciously did not look at the stairway landing. "Uh, *brat*," she finished. "I'd like to make it up to you." She clasped her hands in her lap. "I'm throwing a homecoming party on Saturday night, and you're invited."

So I got suspended from school and my parents disciplined me by taking away my phone. Elena got suspended and her parents let her throw a party.

Life wasn't fair.

"Yeah," I said slowly. "I'm pretty much under house arrest, and a party is kind of the last thing I'd want—"

"But I really want you to come," Elena said. "So we can fix things. I've missed you." Her voice wavered a little bit, and I felt my resolve weaken. "It'd be really small. Just those of us who can't go to homecoming. My mom felt bad that I had to give up the crown, and she thought that was punishment enough. She didn't think I should miss homecoming, too. We'll dress up and have everything exactly like they'll have at the real dance. So it'll just be you, me, Vince, and, well, Logan . . ."

My eyes started to tear up again, despite all my attempts to stem the waterworks.

"Maybe it'd get your mind off things," she said. "You could at least ask your parents. It'll be good for you."

Oh, no. No, it would not. Being forced to watch Vince and Elena have fun while Logan glowered at me from the corner was not my idea of a good time.

"Sorry, my parents took away my phone," I said, relieved to have an excuse. "So I can't call them. But I'll ask them tonight." Yeah, I had no intention of doing that.

Elena knew me too well. She pulled out her phone and said, "That's okay, I have your home phone number programmed in." And she called my parents. While I was right there. So it wasn't like I could put up much of a protest with her looking at me like I was a poor stray animal in need of rescuing.

I shook my head. She'd done this on purpose. I didn't

know whether to feel frustrated or impressed—or both. It was the type of thing she'd pull back when we were on friendlier terms, so I really should have seen it coming. Back then I would have found it inevitable, maybe even charming. I sighed as she handed me the phone, and my dad answered.

Did I want to put up a fight? Really, what was the use? It wasn't like my parents would agree, anyway.

I explained the situation in a minute flat, being sure to use zero inflection, otherwise my dad might think I had schemed with Elena to orchestrate this, and I didn't need my parents on my case any more than they already had been.

"So that's everything," I said, already preparing to sound disappointed when he rejected Elena's plan.

"I think that'd be okay," my dad said instead, shocking me so much that I forgot to keep my face neutral. Elena saw my expression and her face lit up. Well, that was just great. Now I couldn't pretend that my dad had said no.

"Oh . . . Are you sure?"

"Yes. I'll talk to your mother about it, but I'm sure I can convince her. Oh, and I forgot to tell you earlier, I had accounting make out your paycheck. So it's your lucky day. See you in a bit."

My dad hung up, and I didn't know what to do. Elena squealed, pulling me into a hug as she took the phone back. I wasn't prepared for it and froze, unable to return the gesture. Elena seemed genuinely excited, and this only made me more confused.

"I'd really like to work this out," she said when she pulled back.

I didn't speak for almost a full minute. I couldn't. My heart and my brain were at war. I *wanted* to believe her, but we'd both said some pretty awful things, and those were etched in my memory. But there was that glimmer of hope, tantalizing and maybe, just maybe, within reach for the first time in a while.

"Thank you." I took a deep breath, then released it. "I'd like that."

The rest of the evening wrapped up pretty quickly after that. I told Elena I'd try to make her show, too, in a couple of months. I wanted us to actually feel like friends again, but I wouldn't allow myself to really get my hopes up. That was just asking for more disappointment, and who needed that? So instead I welcomed the numbness that seeped through my body.

I made it back home, grabbed my paycheck from my dad, and went up to my room to be alone. I wondered what Logan was doing now. Was he lying in his tree house, looking up, the same way I was lying on my bed, staring at the ceiling? The comparison made me curious, so I booted up my computer to look at his social profiles. Then I remembered my parents had changed the Wi-Fi password and I sighed.

A calendar alert at the bottom of my screen blinked angrily. *Reminder: Final Article for the Competition Due Tonight.* This was the part about school suspensions that no one ever mentioned—I still had to turn in all the work that I'd missed.

I opened up a fresh document on my computer. Then I stared at it for an hour. I groaned and banged my head on my headboard, which was the cue my mom needed to knock on my door.

"How's it going in here?" she asked. I was sitting on my bed with my computer across my lap, so I pulled a pillow across my face and tried to block everything out, muffling my voice in the process.

"Awful. Go away and leave me to my misery."

My mom took that as an invitation, coming in and sitting at the edge of my bed.

"Sometimes you just have to push through," she said, pulling the pillow aside. "Even if it's hard or even if nothing seems right. You've heard the expression, 'It's always darkest before the dawn'?"

Call me crazy, but I had a sneaking suspicion she wasn't talking about my article.

"Things have a way of working out." She leaned over and gave me a kiss on the forehead. "Hang in there, kiddo. If things aren't going your way, sometimes you need to look at them differently."

She stood up. "Trust your gut, and finish the article. It doesn't have to be perfect to be great." She left, and I stared at my computer again, willing it to magically write the sports article for me, my mother's words swirling around my head. *Perfect* and *great*. Those two words had new meaning for me now. Vince was perfect on paper, but Logan was the real deal.

Inspiration hit me then. I couldn't text Logan. I couldn't

go on the internet or email him. My mom had even promised to watch over my shoulder as I submitted this article,
letting me log on to the internet for only two minutes to do
so. But maybe, just maybe, I could explain myself through
the newspaper. The only downside was that everyone at
school would read it, and all my faults would be . . . out there.

I chewed on my lip while I debated my options, but really,
it wasn't like I had much choice.

Technically, it wasn't a perfect fit for the sports column.
But it was kind of about Vince, in a roundabout way, and that
would just have to do.

All my thoughts about life, love, right, and wrong poured
out of me onto the screen.

Of course, writing it out like this made it super obvious
just how wrong I'd been. So that was great. It was also obvious how much I liked Logan.

I wrote about how I'd betrayed pretty much everyone's
trust. Like how Robyn had nothing to do with Vince asking
me out. And I explained the most important truth of all: that
none of Logan's negatives on the pros-and-cons list even mattered to me. At all. I'd tried so hard to convince myself of
Logan's problems that I'd created a monster problem for
myself. Go me.

At the end of the article I made a new list. This one
included every single positive thing I should have mentioned
about Logan the first time. There were a lot.

It wasn't a hard-hitting piece of journalism that uncovered
anyone's juicy secrets, but for the first time in weeks, I was
going to do the right thing.

Before too long, I had a finished article. With my mom watching over my shoulder, I attached the document to an email and hit SEND. Maybe nothing would change, but I could finally live with what I'd done. Tomorrow morning would be better; I was sure of it.

twenty-four

My mom knocked on my door at 7:30 a.m. Thursday morning and said that Mr. Quince was on the phone for me. That was my first clue that things weren't going my way.

"Hello?" I asked, afraid he could hear the hesitation in my voice.

"Good morning, Mia," he said. "I received your article last night. It certainly . . . wasn't what I was expecting."

"Look, I'm sorry, Mr. Quince," I said. "I know it doesn't belong in the sports section. I'll understand if you couldn't print the article."

"Oh, I printed the article," he said. "I just wanted to give you a heads-up, since you won't be in class today when I announce the winner of the contest."

I sat up straighter in bed, clutching the sheets.

"I'm sorry, Mia. This was a great article, but Joey won the internship."

I stopped strangling my sheets and brought my shaking hands back to my lap.

"But you'll still be tallying votes, right?" I asked, hating the waver in my voice. "People who read the paper today will all count until eighth period?"

"Yes," he said, sounding hesitant. "But he's hundreds of page views ahead of everyone else."

I thumped my head against my headboard. That was it then.

"Okay." I swallowed. "Thank you for letting me know."

"Listen, things aren't looking great for the future of our school paper. The administration hasn't made their final decision, but it looks like it'll either be discontinued entirely or we'll go down to a monthly or even quarterly issue. If I work fewer nights formatting and editing the paper, they can use the money for the football team."

I thought he'd already delivered the bad news, but this made his earlier statement seem downright chipper by comparison.

"I'll be telling the rest of the class today, but I thought you should know. Think of this as an opportunity to try new things."

I winced. *Opportunity*. Like that wasn't a spin word we journalists used whenever we wanted to make something sound more positive than it was. Lost your job? It's not a failure, it's an *opportunity*.

Still. I needed to be positive. Sometimes life didn't give you what you wanted, but maybe that was because it had something better in store. If you didn't shoot it in the foot. Or reject it in a janitor's closet.

Someone knocked on our front door, and I started down the stairs. My mom had gotten into the shower after handing me the phone, so I was the lucky one who got to deal with whoever was there. "Thanks again for letting me know," I said, reaching the bottom step. "Someone's at our door, so I need to go . . ."

"Oh sure, sure," he said. "Have a great day. And really, you should be proud. Your article was really good." *Right. Just not good enough to win.*

I hung up and opened the door. I couldn't help but smile when I saw Robyn on the porch, even if I'd just received terrible news about the journalism internship and the fate of our paper.

"Hey, did I wake you up?" she asked, going in for a hug.

"Nah," I said, hugging her back. "Mr. Quince did that already."

"Speaking of Mr. Quince, so there I was minding my own business, walking into homeroom a little early, when he shoves a paper in my hands and tells me to read the front page."

Robyn handed me the paper in question. There it was: my article, front and center. Not in the sports section at all.

My stomach fluttered as I unfolded it. Underneath mine was an article by Elena, and wonder of wonders, *this* article actually seemed sincere. At least the title was. *Top Ten Reasons I'm an Idiot*. Chances were pretty good I was going to read it this time. Robyn raised her eyebrows and stepped inside.

"So you're playing hooky?" I asked, closing the door. "You can't pretend you were sick if Mr. Quince already saw you."

"He's the one who told me to come."

Weird. I'd just gotten off the phone with him. Why would he send Robyn here?

"Oh! I have something for you," I said, suddenly remembering. I turned on my heel and ran back upstairs to grab the envelope of money from the paycheck I'd cashed. It wasn't a whole lot, but hopefully it would at least make up for what I'd done.

I ran back down the stairs, catching myself from falling by grabbing onto the railing, and handed the envelope to Robyn. Her eyes widened as she opened it.

"How did you get this? I don't need—"

"Yes, you do," I said. "It's my fault you haven't gotten a car yet, and I want to make it right. I wrote some website copy for my dad's company, no big deal. Don't you dare think about trying to give it back."

She smiled and gave a slow nod.

"Thank you." She pulled me into another hug. "It's really great," she said, my hair muffling half her words.

"Are we good?" I asked when she pulled away.

"We already were," she said firmly, walking into the living room, with me trailing behind. "You're my best friend, and I know your heart was in the right place. Plus I've gotten more applications today than ever before from people who never would have even known about my matching business if it weren't for your article. So don't worry about me. What about everyone else? I mean, when I read your article, you made it sound like you think everyone still hates you and you've ruined your life forever."

She threw herself onto our couch, fluffing the pillows behind her head. I sank into the chair across from her.

"Well," I said. "Yes and no." She cast me a quizzical glance, and I fished around for the best way to say what I was thinking.

"Elena doesn't hate me anymore. Or Vince, I don't think. But Logan? Yeah, he pretty much thinks I'm the devil. I've had nothing but radio silence from him." And it still hurt. Like stepping on Legos every time I thought of his name. Maybe my article would explain things, but the chances that Logan would read it were worse than my odds at fantasy football. Too bad I hadn't considered that last night when I'd written it.

"Elena doesn't hate you? That's new. Give me all the juicy details." Was it just my imagination, or was she fingering the flap of the money envelope in a nervous way? And why did she keep pushing the conversation back to me?

"Well, apparently she and Vince are dating now, so all is forgiven."

"What, just like that?"

"Sort of," I said. "I think it helped when she found out about the email, because then Vince's actions made sense to her, and it's not like she could be mad at me just for having similar taste in guys."

Robyn nodded, looking entirely too comfortable on my couch. Like she was never planning on going back to school. Like maybe my article had made things awkward for her and now she was hiding out, and it was all my fault. Was that why she was acting so weird? Was she here as some kind of escape?

"Are you only here because Mr. Quince wanted you to give me the paper? I could have read it online," I said.

"I'm touched you care so much about why I skipped class." She brought a hand to her chest and grinned. Then, seeming to realize I wouldn't let her off the hook, she sighed. "Mr. Quince thought you might need moral support, since everyone at school will be reading such a personal article. That's why I didn't call. I wanted to see you and make sure you were handling all this okay." Robyn bit her lip and looked back at the ceiling. "And that's not the only reason I came. But you might hate me after I tell you."

I racked my brain, trying to think of any reason Robyn might land on my naughty list.

"When Mr. Quince first mentioned the paper was in trouble, I began thinking of options," Robyn said. "Maybe my Dear Robyn column isn't the most revolutionary idea, but I wanted to prove that *all* parts of journalism have a purpose and that they shouldn't shut down the paper." She took a deep breath before continuing.

"I found out about a grant available to high school students.

One that pays admittance to a summer journalism workshop in New York. And I submitted an application article. Well, more of a thesis, really. It was twenty pages. Mr. Quince gave the teacher's referral. I hoped that if I got it, the school would see how it wouldn't have been possible without all my experience on the paper."

"That's pretty great," I said, failing to see how Robyn thought this could all end badly. Though, to be honest, I was a little hurt she hadn't mentioned the grant to me so I could apply, too. Then again, with the past couple of weeks I'd had, there wouldn't have been any time for a twenty-page thesis.

Robyn shook her head.

"The essay was about you."

"What?" I tried to catch her eye, but Robyn was looking anywhere but at me.

She pulled a couch pillow over her face.

"I wrote about advice columns, and the ethic responsibility journalists have toward their readers." She pulled the cushion aside and finally looked at me. "Ironically, I did the most unethical thing by writing it without your knowledge. I wrote about your relationship mess and how I, as Dear Robyn, played a role. I encouraged Logan to play hard to get, but I need you to know that I really, honestly thought it would help."

Logan's words came crashing back into my mind, how he'd thought he'd ruined Robyn's article by kissing me. Now all those times Robyn had been secretive were beginning to make sense. Why she'd refused to show me the article she

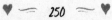

was working on. Why she hadn't told me her summer plans when all the rest of us were vying for the internship.

I'd been so clueless. But Logan had known, at least to some extent. Because he had asked Elena out, simply because Robyn had told him to. To make me jealous. During community service, he said kissing me had never been part of Robyn's plan. Then he said he was done being manipulated by her and wanted to be honest. I wanted to ask Robyn if he'd known the article focused on me, rather than just matchmaking in general, but she kept talking before I could even process all the emotions dancing through me.

"I tried to be an impartial observer, but sometimes I couldn't help myself. I'm so sorry. I took your pain and turned it into my application article, and I feel really bad about it. Mr. Quince made me promise to tell you all this, because, well, I heard back from the grant board, and I've been accepted into the summer workshop."

She gave a tiny *surprise!* kind of smile, throwing out jazz hands.

"And this twenty-page thesis will be printed where . . . ?"

"No, no, it won't be printed." Robyn sat up with the force of her declaration. "Only the panel judges read it, I promise. But I'll send you a copy so you can read it. Please don't hate me."

I nodded, still processing everything.

"I don't hate you," I said slowly, as if testing the words to see if they felt true. But really, knowing the article wasn't going to be printed anywhere made my decision easy.

"Because, I guess, you didn't really do anything that I wouldn't have done myself. And I'm happy for you that you got the grant." It was the truth. And it was the least I could do after everything that had happened.

Robyn came over and hugged me then. The air felt clear between us, and I sighed in relief.

"Are you going to go back to school?" I asked her.

"Maybe. Maybe not." She sighed as she went back to the couch. "Think your parents would mind if I crashed here for a bit?"

My mom came downstairs then, so I let her handle that question.

"Robyn!" she said. "Aren't you supposed to be in school?"

"Playing hooky from homeroom today," Robyn said, and I cringed, waiting for my mom's response. Most— scratch that, *all* my perfectionist tendencies came directly from her. And if my mom thought Robyn was a negative influence . . . Well, let's just say we could forget about seeing each other. Like, ever again. But then again, Robyn wasn't the suspended one.

"I'm here on official business. Mr. Quince cleared it with the office."

My mom pursed her lips. "Well, okay. I have to go to work, though, so I can't stick around to make sure you go back. Don't stay too long." She'd been a lot more lenient since my reconciliation meeting at Elena's, though she hadn't given me back my phone. I had a feeling I could kiss that goodbye forever.

"Thanks, Mrs. Taylor. You're the best," Robyn said, and my mom smiled as she picked up the keys.

"All right. I'm off. You two behave. Mia, I'm leaving you my phone so you can reach me if you go out. If you do, be home for dinner at six." She left, and Robyn turned to face me.

"She's pretty easygoing considering you were suspended . . ." Robyn trailed off, waiting for me to explain.

"Yeah," I said. "Elena's mom called and told her the food fight was Elena's fault, so my parents have backed off a lot. They're not blaming me for things."

"I'm glad you're patching things up with Elena," Robyn said.

"Oh! That reminds me," I said. "You're coming to her homecoming party Saturday night, right? You can bring a date." I gave her my best puppy-dog eyes. "Like maybe Joey?" I'd never brought him up before, at least not this bluntly, and Robyn narrowed her eyes in warning. Well, that certainly wasn't the way to get what I wanted.

"Please!" I swallowed. "I won't be able to stand the awkwardness if I'm forced to make small talk with Logan all night." I hurried on before Robyn could notice the way my voice caught on his name. "It's supposed to be just the people who were suspended, but I know she'll invite more, and I'll be the social outcast hanging out by myself." I took a deep breath and tried to plaster on a smile. It came out wobbly. "Please say you'll come? You guys have been talking again lately, too, right?"

"Hmm," Robyn said. "If that's what you want, then I guess I could make an appearance."

"Thank you, thank you. You're the best," I said. I took a deep breath. "It's nice to have a friend in my corner, what with the internship going to Joey, the paper probably shutting down, and Logan . . ." I couldn't finish saying it.

Robyn fixed me with a solid stare.

"You'll work things out with Logan, you know. Have you heard from him at all?"

I shook my head and blinked rapidly so I wouldn't cry.

"Well, that doesn't mean much," she said, pursing her lips. "You've been cut off from the world. He doesn't know your home phone number, does he?"

"I've already tried calling him from it. He didn't answer."

Robyn waved her hand in the air. "Maybe he's still a little mad then. But your article has to soften him up a little."

I gave her a weak smile. "Yeah. Too bad Logan doesn't read the paper."

"It doesn't matter," she said. "You two are meant to be together. I've been in this business for a while. I can read the signs."

"That's a nice thought," I said. Even though at this point, I knew it was a lost cause.

"Well, you know what they say," she said. "'The course of true love never did run smooth.'"

twenty-five

I sighed. It must have sounded pathetic, because Robyn sat up and scrutinized me so intensely, I felt like a fish in a clear bowl. "Okay, enough with the sad stuff," she said, standing up and putting her hands on her hips. "You know what? I think you need to get out."

"I agree," I said. "Where should we go?"

"The first place you should go is the shower and then we'll talk when you don't smell like depression." She waved her hand at me, and I grudgingly made my way upstairs. Leave it to Robyn to boss me around in my own home.

She was right, however. The shower made me feel like I hadn't been camping under a rock, and brushing my teeth added another point to the happiness scale. Looking in the mirror, I actually looked like myself, so that was a plus.

I came downstairs to see Robyn raiding the kitchen.

"Don't you guys have anything that isn't fat-free anymore?" she asked over her shoulder, her head buried in the cupboard.

"The second cabinet to the right has my secret stash of chips and cookies. Behind the broken toaster. They're store-bought and a little stale, but the alternative is the black-bean brownies my mom made."

Robyn made a face as she opened the cupboard. "Black beans and brownies are two things that should never be put together," she said.

"I couldn't agree more."

"All right." She grabbed a cookie from the package and turned to face me. "What place makes you the happiest?"

"The beach," I answered automatically. "A sunny, sandy one." The thought made me think of Elena, with her dreams of Hollywood. This didn't bring as much of a pang as I thought it would, and I smiled.

Robyn took a bite and spoke with her mouth full. "I mean somewhere that's within driving distance, silly. Where was the last place you had a good time?"

I sat at the table and tried to remember what happiness really felt like. Sure, it felt good to have showered, but I still was hollow on the inside. Like one of those chocolate Easter bunnies that disappointed me every year when I bit into it and found out it wasn't solid.

"The Pier, I guess," I said. "It's where Logan took me on our first date." I paused. "Well, kind of our only real date."

"Great. You can go to the Pier and eat your weight in cotton candy while I go back to school."

"What?" I said. "No, you can't ditch me. We're going together."

She walked over and placed her hands on my shoulders.

"I have a few things I have to take care of. But I promise I'll meet you there after school. Okay?"

"What's so important that you have to ditch me in my time of need?" I batted my eyelashes and pouted.

"Spanish," she said. "I have a test in about half an hour. Plus there's a bake sale going on today, and I heard Joey made his famous cake-batter muddy buddies."

I sighed. No one could compete with that. Especially because Joey was involved. "Fine. Be that way. But if you're not there by four o'clock, I swear I'll tell your little brothers the password to your computer and you can deal with the consequences. And you'd better bring me some muddy buddies."

She smiled in triumph and slung her bag over one shoulder. "As you wish."

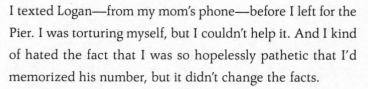

I texted Logan—from my mom's phone—before I left for the Pier. I was torturing myself, but I couldn't help it. And I kind of hated the fact that I was so hopelessly pathetic that I'd memorized his number, but it didn't change the facts.

Logan didn't answer.

I checked the phone every twenty seconds. What use was

a phone if Logan wouldn't respond to my texts? Even though the phone said my text had been delivered, those three little dots that showed he was writing a reply never popped up.

I stared at the screen. Were we over for good? Would he ever speak to me again?

I drove by his house on my way to the Pier. As long as I was torturing myself, I might as well do a good job of it. I pulled off to the side of the road and debated whether I should knock on his door. What would I say?

Hello, Logan, remember me? The girl who broke your heart and then pureed it in a blender?

No. As much as I wanted to knock, I couldn't bring myself to open my car door. My hands were frozen, like my eyes, which were glued to his house.

A movement in the front window caught my attention. Logan's face appeared for the briefest of moments before he walked out of sight. My breath caught, and my knuckles tightened on the wheel. I hadn't seen him since that disastrous day at community service two days ago. I resisted the urge to duck in my seat. There was an 80 percent chance that Logan had already seen me. The window looked directly onto the street.

Option one: Go knock. He'd probably seen me, anyway.

Option two: Drive away and don't look back.

I checked the phone again but still no text from Logan.

It always seemed so climactic in movies whenever someone banged their head against the steering wheel. But I couldn't even muster up the energy. Because all that I felt was hollow. Hollow, empty, and numb. I'd briefly felt better, when Robyn had been around. But now, on my own again? I could only feel the pain.

My finger hovered over the numbers on my mom's phone. *Why don't you call him? Scared?* my inner thoughts taunted.

Yes, I replied.

But I did it anyway. I input the numbers, hit the green phone icon, and listened to it ring. While it was ringing, I tried to see through the window. I knew he was home, and I couldn't think of any reason why he wouldn't have his phone on him.

But he didn't answer.

I hung up when his voicemail clicked on, too defeated to do anything else.

I had my answer. Logan really wanted nothing to do with me. Even if he didn't answer calls from unknown numbers, my text had explained that it was me. I went ahead and deleted the text in question, so my mom wouldn't see. While she'd loaned me the phone, I was pretty sure texting Logan wasn't exactly encouraged. At the time, it had seemed worth the potential blowup, should my mom ever find out. But if he didn't even answer . . .

Logan was home, but he wasn't answering. Those were the facts. Any reporter worth their salt would call it like it was and move on already. So how come I couldn't accept it? How stupid could I get?

I put my car in drive.

twenty-six

The Ferris wheel seemed different during the day. Taller somehow. Scarier. I could actually see how high up I was, the ground disappearing with every rotation. I'd paid the worker ten bucks to let me ride as long as I wanted, but I was only a few minutes into it and I was already regretting my impulse. Too bad I'd already visited all the booths. There wasn't anything left for me to do while I waited for Robyn.

I tried to settle back in the empty gondola seat. The metal was hard and uncomfortable, making me think of how much better it'd been to lean against Logan while he held my hand. But I didn't want to think about Logan. Or the way his hair swung into his eyes, or how I felt when he teased me, or any of those thoughts that made me miss him more than I already did. His rejection left a crater-size hole that no amount of cotton candy could fill.

The Ferris wheel had been a bad idea. I shouldn't have come to the Pier in the first place.

My gondola stopped at the bottom, and despite my second thoughts about the whole thing, I was ready to give the worker a piece of my mind for accepting my money but breaking his promise. That is until I looked up to see Logan standing there beside the worker.

At first, I couldn't believe it. Thinking of him had made me hallucinate. It couldn't be real.

Logan. Here. My brain wasn't making sense of what was happening, but he was smiling, so that had to be a good thing, right?

He looked good, too. How was I supposed to play things cool when he looked that good? Curse him and his tousled hair. His gray Henley that hugged his frame and made him seem irresistibly toned. I didn't need those things right now.

Correction: I really needed all those things—as close to me as possible.

"Mind if I join you?" Logan asked as the worker opened my bar to let him in. What was I supposed to say? And why wasn't I saying anything? *Speak, Mia!* Oh goodness, now I was talking to myself like a dog. Or thinking to myself, rather. That was even worse. What was wrong with me? My cheeks felt flushed, and I nervously scooted over so there'd be enough room for him to sit. By me. He gave me a hesitant, uncertain smile. Maybe he didn't know that my answer was, and always would be, yes. My pulse was beating so hard, he could probably feel its reverberations from my palm to where it touched the seat.

Logan sat down, and the worker lowered the bar once again and sent us on our way. We slowly rose up to the sky, and as we did, my heart seemed to rise, too. The air seemed different with him here. It was charged with energy, like one spark could set off something either amazing or terrible. Only time would tell which. The anticipation was so intense, I couldn't figure out what to do with my hands. They seemed awkward on the seat, so I moved them to the bar. But their shaking was so obvious that I shoved them under my legs, hoping Logan wouldn't notice.

"How'd you know I was here?" I finally asked when the silence grew to be too much.

Logan put one arm on the back of the seat, and my brain went into hyperdrive, analyzing whether he thought of it as a friendly gesture. It was technically draped over the chair and not my shoulders, but if I leaned back just a little, we'd be touching. I couldn't bring myself to do it, no matter how much I wanted to. I was frozen now, waiting for him to realize his mistake and withdraw his arm.

"A little birdie told me," he said. "A Robyn."

"Ah," I said. I guess I shouldn't have been surprised that she would stop by Logan's on her way to school. It was a wonder we hadn't run into each other.

"I tried calling you," I said. What I really wanted to ask was *Why did you ignore me?* But I couldn't bring myself to say it.

"My parents took my phone away," he said.

I hadn't known that. But man, did it make me hope. Because if he hadn't been ignoring me . . .

"Robyn told me I had to read today's paper," Logan said. "Specifically, an article on the front page written by a mutual friend."

Friend. He'd said *friend*. I mean, it wasn't like he would have said *mutual girlfriend*. So I shouldn't start panicking. Yet. But I was definitely panicking. Why had Logan said *friend*? Was he only repeating what Robyn had told him? He had to know I was analyzing every single word that came from his lips. Oh no. Now I was thinking about his lips. I stared at them and wondered what it'd feel like to have them on mine right now. Of course, that wouldn't happen. Because Logan had said *friend*.

I muffled that part of my brain and tried to remember what Logan had just said. Something about my article. Oh no, what if he hated it?

"You read it?" I asked, too surprised to worry whether my tone offended him. "But you never read the paper."

"Sometimes I make exceptions." He nudged me.

A warmth blossomed in my chest at that, like fuzzy slippers in the morning. He'd read the paper. For me.

"I'm so sorry about that pros-and-cons list." I swallowed. "It was old, and I wasn't even writing the truth. I was just trying so desperately to pretend like I was right, and I never meant to hurt you."

He gave me a weak smile. "I'm sorry I reacted so badly. It caught me off-guard."

"You had every right to react the way you did," I said, shaking my head.

"Yeah, I guess I wasn't ready for someone to say just how ridiculous my hair looks. Let me see . . . 'like a wannabe Harry Styles,' isn't that right?" He grinned, and I fought the urge to reach out and touch the hair in question.

"It's grown on me," I said, shrugging a shoulder. "Who knew I had a thing for boy bands?"

"And you can live with my being 'permanently attached to my camera like it's a baby'? Your words, not mine. Because I will have you know, I don't always carry it with me. Like right now. I totally proved you wrong." He held up his free hand to show it was empty, and I wanted to hold it in mine. I bit my lip instead.

"That, too. I am definitely okay with that."

"And you said you don't think I'm serious. About anything?" His voice dropped low, sending shivers up my arms. He caught my gaze, and I was frozen to the spot, unable to move for fear of breaking the spell. "I can prove you wrong about that, too."

"So, so sorry about that one," I said, my words barely loud enough to carry between us.

"It was a mistake, Mia." His eyes were intent on mine. "It happens. You didn't mean any harm by it, just like you didn't know how to fix things after you emailed Vince."

"I'm sorry about that, too," I said. I sounded like a broken record, but I couldn't help it.

"You might have said that—about a bazillion times in

your article. But I've had some time to think about every-thing, and I can see why you did it. I'm good." He nudged me with the hand draped across the back of the seat, pulling me slightly closer. I smiled and scooted over.

Still leaving his arm behind me, Logan reached across with his other and intertwined his fingers with mine. It felt so good, I momentarily forgot what we were talking about. Then he stroked my hand with his thumb, and I was so far gone I couldn't have come back if I tried.

"So we're . . . ?" I trailed off. I wanted to ask if that meant we were officially together, but I didn't want to risk him say-ing no.

Logan's mouth curved up.

"We're good," he said. "More than good. We're great."

I was mush. Pure and simple. There was nothing else Logan could have said that would have made me more gooey.

Logan slid his arm down so it settled around my shoul-ders, and I relaxed against him. How could I have thought this seat was uncomfortable before? I didn't ever want to leave.

He kissed my temple, and sunlight warmed every part of my body.

He let go of my hand to cup my face. I felt my pulse speed up in anticipation of what would happen next. He leaned in even closer, and I could feel his breath on my skin.

"Mia," he said, his eyes focused on mine. "I'm going to kiss you now."

"Hmm." I pretended to consider, but really, I would

probably burst if he didn't kiss me soon. "A kiss at the top of a Ferris wheel? I don't know. Isn't that too cliché?"

He didn't bother answering me, and for that, I was grateful. He closed the distance between us and placed his lips gently on mine. His kiss was soft and slow, a promise that we'd have all the time in the world. A promise I could believe in.

My fingers tangled in his hair, and I pulled him closer to me. He wound one arm around my back and placed the other at my waist. He deepened the kiss, and I gladly reciprocated. His kiss warmed me from the inside out, and despite the autumn wind, I could have stayed in that moment forever. Never had it felt so right to have someone's lips on mine.

After a few moments, he pulled away and rested his forehead on mine. Our breath mingled in the air, and we both smiled. His hand stroked my cheek, and I leaned into it.

"I hope you don't mind, but I asked Robyn if you guys could hang out some other time," he said. "She didn't seem too sorry about breaking her promise to meet you here."

"I don't mind." I smiled, and he kissed me again.

We rode the Ferris wheel for a long time.

twenty-seven

Elena's house lit up the entire street.

"I thought this wasn't supposed to be a big deal," Logan said as we stepped onto a porch decorated with hanging stars. He looked super good in his all-black tux, and I was incredibly grateful that Elena had insisted we all dress up for her fake homecoming party. And that the tux rental place had a no-cancellations policy. My dad had taken pictures back at my house, with Logan's camera. Of course, Logan adjusted all the settings and told my dad exactly where to stand and how to frame the shot, so maybe they'd actually turn out okay. I was totally going to plaster them all over my room the second they got printed.

"Yeah, well, you know Elena," I said as I rang the doorbell. Logan caught my hand on its way down and wove his fingers through mine. It sent tingles up my arm. When Elena opened the door, it was to see me gazing up at Logan with a pathetically goofy grin on my face.

"Well, well, what do we have here?" She tsked. "I thought you were supposed to reserve this kind of behavior for your own porch at the end of a night."

"I, ummm . . ." I stammered.

Then she squealed and pulled me into a hug. "I'm so happy for you two! Tonight will be awesome. Mia, you look amazing. I hope you don't mind that I invited a few more people. Most of them are just stopping by for a minute before going to the homecoming dance."

I turned to Logan and gave him my *I told you so* face. He chuckled and nodded, admitting I was right. Of course, I'd had an inkling of her plans when she'd mentioned her party in her last gossip column.

Elena led us inside, and I saw some people from school milling around, dancing to the music coming from Elena's sound system. There were only about twenty people, but I had a feeling the crowd would only grow as the night went on. Athens High wasn't exactly known for its killer dances, so more people would bounce here as they grew fed up with soft hits and dress codes enforced with honest-to-goodness rulers. With Logan at my side, though, I found I wasn't bothered by the extra people. He wrapped an arm around my waist, and I leaned into him, taking advantage of the opportunity to breathe in his scent.

Elena brought Vince over to where we stood, and I braced myself for the inevitable awkwardness. It seemed like everyone in the room tensed, as if waiting for another fight to break out.

"Hey, man," Logan said, surprising me by smiling.

"I see you've stopped chasing my girlfriend," Vince said. He put an arm across Elena's shoulders, and she poked him in the side.

"I see you've stopped chasing mine," Logan answered. Vince smirked and extended his fist toward Logan, who bumped it with his own.

And that seemed to be it. I'd never understood how guys could do that. I mean, they could easily put anything behind them as long as they each got to throw a couple of punches. It made absolutely no sense. The room returned to a normal noise level, and people went back to their own conversations.

"I'm glad you guys came," Elena said. "And that you're together. Mia, Logan is lucky to have you."

"Hmm," I said, looking up at him. "More like I'm the one who's lucky to have him." Really, really lucky. About a lot of things.

Elena smiled, and she actually looked really happy for me. It might have been an act, but it was enough to give me hope we'd be able to move past all this eventually. She seemed to be thinking the same thing.

"Mia, I know things have been . . . rocky between us lately, but I promise I'm going to try to make it up to you. First, by pointing you to the kitchen. My mom let me buy your favorite cheesecake."

Okay, forget about the five pounds I knew I'd put on

during my moping period. There was no way I could resist the siren call of cheesecake. Especially with the weird diet my mom was enforcing at our house. I'd eaten most of my comfort stash over the last few days, so this might be the last time I'd be able to ingest copious amounts of sugar for a while. Plus, going to another room eliminated the need for awkward chitchat with Elena.

"Thanks, Elena," I said as Logan steered me away, toward the kitchen. He knew me too well.

The kitchen was empty at the moment, and I took an extra-large slice. I'll admit, though, it was hard to focus on cheesecake with the way Logan was looking at me. He took a fork from the counter and stole a bite from my plate.

"You're lucky you're so cute," I teased. "People have paid dearly for lesser offenses."

"Mmmm," he said around a mouthful of cheesecake. He swallowed and licked his lips, which drew my attention to his mouth. "I'm glad you think I'm cute then." He put one arm behind me and leaned close.

He kissed me then, and his kisses were better than cheesecake. Especially when he put an arm on either side of me, pinning me to the counter. His body was so close to mine, I could feel him breathe, which made me deliriously happy. For the first time in a long time, all of me felt full. Maybe Joey had won the internship and the future of the paper was uncertain, but my dreams didn't end there. I was realizing there were lots of options, some I'd never considered. Like Logan. I wound my arms around his neck and focused on pouring all my emotions into the kiss. If anyone could see me then, I was pretty sure I was glowing.

We hid out in the kitchen for a while. When we emerged, I spotted Robyn in the crowd.

"You came!" I said, and hugged her. "So have you and Elena talked?"

"Yeah, I guess we're okay now that she knows I had nothing to do with your mess." Robyn elbowed me in the side. "Plus she said she bought cheesecake, so I guess all is forgiven."

There was a reason Robyn and I were best friends. "Hey," I said, remembering the last time we'd spoken on Thursday morning. "You still owe me muddy buddies."

"Ah, but I delivered something so much better," she said, tilting her head toward Logan, who placed a kiss on my temple. She did have a point there.

"True. Thank you for telling Logan to read the article."

Robyn smirked, placing her hands on her hips. "You two be good now. I need to go find some other lost souls in need of matchmaking."

"You didn't come with a date?" I asked. Sure, she hadn't mentioned asking Joey, but she was Cupid. Why didn't she use her skills to help herself?

"Why would I need a date when I have so much work to do?" Robyn asked, flashing me a grin. Was it just me, or did her smile falter a bit?

"You know what they say, 'always a matchmaker, never a . . .'" I trailed off, because I had no idea where I was going with that comment.

Robyn just looked at me, clearly unimpressed with my half metaphor.

"I think I'm good. Okay then," she said, shrugging. "I'm off."

She gave me a wave and disappeared into the crowd, leaving me standing with Logan. Maybe I sucked at playing matchmaker, but there was still one person I felt could benefit from me stepping in. One day. Soon.

Logan put his arms around me, and I leaned my head against his chest. There were other couples dancing around us, but it felt like we were all alone.

"I think I'm going to look up some online student-run papers," I told Logan. He pulled back to see my face, his arms still encircled about my waist.

"Yeah?"

"Yeah." There were multiple ways to achieve one dream. Robyn had taught me that by applying for her unconventional grant. "I still want to be a journalist, even if things don't work out at the school paper. This way I can still get experience for college applications. Hopefully I can find some papers that will take me." Closing one door didn't mean I was out of windows, after all. I'd thought that before, with Vince, and look where that had gotten me.

"You'll get in. You'll be amazing," he said, pulling me close. "I even promise to read your articles."

We gently swayed to the music, and I let all other thoughts go.

For the first time in weeks, everything felt right.

"Want to know a secret?" Logan whispered in my ear. I

nodded against his chest, not wanting to put any distance between us. My mom would have said we were dancing too close, but to me, it felt perfect. "You're my favorite," he said. His breath tickled my cheek, and I looked up to see his chocolate eyes soaking me in.

"Your favorite what?" I asked.

"Everything. You're my favorite everything."

I reached up and put my arms around his neck, bringing his head close to mine. Then I kissed him. Again. Because I could.

acknowledgments

I'd like to bear-hug everyone who helped make this book a reality. But since that would be super awkward, I'll settle with thanking them here.

First of all, thank you to my publisher, Swoon Reads, for believing in my book even when it was a hot mess. Jean Feiwel, you took a chance on me, and I'll be forever grateful. It's changed my life in the best of ways.

My editor, Kat Brzozowski, who had the vision to take the rags of my book and turn it into a beautiful ball gown. This Cinderella wouldn't have been possible without you. (No, seriously. Not. Possible.)

The team at Swoon Reads/Macmillan is amazing! Huge thanks go to Lauren Scobell, Emily Settle, and Holly West for being so supportive and helpful. The Swoon Reads interns, Shania Ballard and Ruqayyah Daud—both of you have such bright futures ahead of you. Ilana Worrell, the production editor, and

Kim Waymer, the production manager, you are rock stars! Thanks go to my copyeditor, Valerie Shea, who has such an amazing eye for detail. Madison Furr, thank you for all your hard work with the publicity and marketing of my book. Also Liz Dresner, the cover designer, and Emily Osbourne, the cover artist—I can't stop staring at your beautiful creation. Marketing and publicity, thank you for all the work you've done for me and my book.

Major kudos go to my family. My husband, Brad, who put up with all my random plot questions, even when it was incredibly late and he just wanted to go to sleep. He cooks, cleans, runs errands, and is generally a superhero in every sense of the word. I can't imagine life without him. My son, who will happily watch television so I can write and doesn't complain when I feed him yet another peanut-butter-and-honey sandwich because I can't cook—like, at all. My mom and dad, who never doubted that this day would finally come. They always encouraged me to chase my dreams and kept listening, no matter how many times I struggled in the journey.

And I can't have an acknowledgments section without thanking my fantabulous critique partners. Kelly Lyman, I can't even count how many times you've read this book, but I know it's gotten old by now. I love you to pieces. Brookie Cowles, thank you for supporting me every step of the way and celebrating each milestone with me. I'm so lucky to have you in my life.

And last but *definitely* not least—you! Thank you for reading my book, whoever you may be. Books can't exist without readers, and I'm so happy you took time out of your busy life to read mine. Thank you, thank you, thank you! Awkward hugs all around!

DID YOU KNOW...

readers like you helped to get this book published?

Join our book-obsessed community and help us discover awesome new writing talent.

1

Write it.

Share your original YA manuscript.

2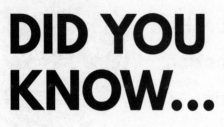

Read it.

Discover bright new bookish talent.

3

Share it.

Discuss, rate, and share your faves.

4

Love it.

Help us publish the books you love.

Share your own manuscript or dive between the pages at **swoonreads.com** or by downloading the **Swoon Reads app.**

**Check out more books
chosen for publication
by readers like you.**

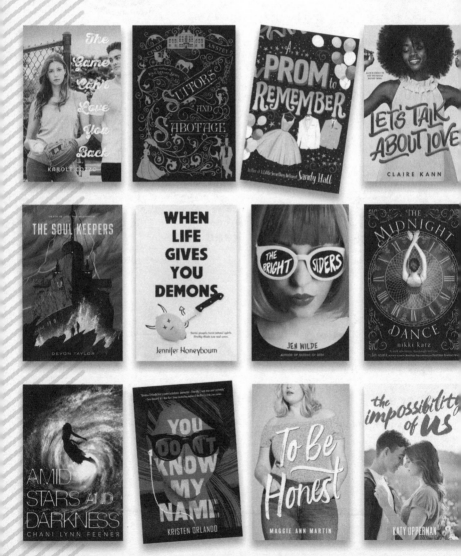